SISTER OF EMBERS & ECHOES

Rogue Ethereal - Book 4

ANNIE ANDERSON

SISTER of EMBERS & ECHOES
Rogue Ethereal Book 4
International Bestselling Author
Annie Anderson

Edited by Angela Sanders
Cover Design by Danielle Fine

www.annieande.com
Official Annie Anderson Newsletter

For my sisters.
From Hell and back and every road in between…
I'll always walk that path with you.

"A man from hell is not afraid of hot ashes."

— DOROTHY GILMAN

BOOKS BY ANNIE ANDERSON

ROGUE ETHEREAL SERIES

Woman of Blood & Bone

Daughter of Souls & Silence

Lady of Madness & Moonlight

Sister of Embers & Echoes

Priestess of Storms & Stone

PHOENIX RISING SERIES

Flame Kissed

Death Kissed

Fate Kissed

Shade Kissed

Sight Kissed

SHELTER ME SERIES

Seeking Sanctuary

Reaching Refuge

Chasing Cover

Seek You Find Me

(A Romantic Suspense Newsletter Serial)

CHAPTER ONE

My eyes narrowed over the rim of my teacup. My grandmother crossed her legs, matching my glare as she sipped her own tea. In all likelihood, she was holding in a laugh. Bernadette had seen oceans rise and fall, empires crumble to dust, entire civilizations wiped from the face of the earth. As one of the first demons in Hell, nothing short of a full-blown apocalypse was going to phase her.

Especially not my paltry little glare.

Fair enough.

Uncrossing my legs, I folded them underneath me, sucking down another sip of my tea as I settled deeper into the overstuffed armchair. I wasn't a big tea kind of person, but the herbal blend I'd concocted in a fit of nerves last week seemed to be growing on me. I'd been doing a lot of things like that—things that Maria would have done herself if she'd just freaking wake up.

"I'm not setting foot in Aether until Maria wakes up, and that's final."

Final.

Like that word ever stopped my grandmother. I was pretty sure if she had even a single shred less class, she'd have given the Fates the old double middle-finger salute while telling them to kiss her ass.

That last bit might just be wishful thinking on my part. At least it was amusing to think about.

"It's been a week, Maxima," Bernadette chided softly, her voice full of understanding, but her message clear. I couldn't wait much longer to interrogate Elias. The Fates were running out of patience, and I was running out of time.

"Have they gotten anything out of him at all?" I asked, unable to keep my gaze from shifting from Bernadette to Maria's closed bedroom door.

I didn't like being on this side of it. I didn't like that I wasn't watching her.

I didn't like that I couldn't figure out a way to help.

A week ago, Elias Flynn tried to use my sister as a sacrifice by offering her up to a demon as a host. Bernadette helped me stop him, but Maria still wasn't awake. The longer her sleep lasted, the more I realized we might not have been as successful as I once thought.

If we were successful at all.

"He isn't telling us anything we didn't know already. Della refuses to go without you, and very few witches are willing to do memory spells. Especially since he is no more magical than a human now."

I pursed my lips but refused to feel guilty. Elias used to be a very gifted moon witch. I say *"used to be"* because I turned off his magic like a kitchen faucet. I had a feeling I wasn't supposed to be able to do that. And since I was the only person I knew who was actually able to do that bit of magic, I wasn't a hundred percent on how it actually worked.

"I'm not sorry for nulling him. It was either that or kill him."

Elias wasn't the first person I'd nulled. I did the same to a shifter named Finn. Finn had deserved it, too, but no one deserved to have his powers stripped more than Elias.

"No one is saying you did the wrong thing, Maxima. But there are realities to this situation you need to be aware of. I'm not going to sugarcoat it just because you decided to take a holiday in the middle of a shit storm."

Bernadette uncrossed her legs, planted her feet, and stood. Her visage of an aging beauty slipped for a moment, showing her true face underneath. I always tended to forget that she put on the façade of an older woman rather than keep the unchanging one she was born with. And to see the face that she tried so desperately to keep hidden meant she was well and truly done with my bullshit.

I was acting like a child with no responsibilities instead of the four-hundred-year-old newly minted Leader of the Keys. Other than order takeout and watch my sister sleep, I had done little else besides tooling around my greenhouse and trying not to panic.

"She is in this mess because of me," I whispered, trying not to let all my sorrow fall from my mouth at once.

"No, Maria is in this mess because of a moon witch with an ax to grind. Maria is stuck in that bed because I didn't do my job of keeping you and yours safe. You want a pity party? Well, you're going to have to pass some around, kid. Put the blame on the prat who deserves it and find out what else he knows. That's the only way we're going to find out who else is with him. Letting him sit in that cell is just asking for the guilty parties to gut him in his sleep to keep him quiet."

Well, she wasn't wrong.

"Fine." I sighed, resignation pulling at every letter in that single syllable. "I'll go in. Tomorrow, though. Let me get an actual night of rest, and I'll go into Aether in the morning."

Bernadette huffed, but it was a good-natured one, so I shot her a smile.

"So now that that little drama is over, tell me about that big box of fighting leathers just sitting on your coffee table. I read the card. You made a deal with Alistair Quinn? Do I even want to know why?"

I thought back to the night I accidentally summoned a demon to my casting room. Directly from Hell. An act that should have taken an entire coven of witches with *not* a little bit of magic to accomplish. Bernadette would be the least likely to judge me for what happened with Alistair.

Probably.

"I may have accidentally summoned him into a circle. From Hell. In exchange for him not ratting me out, I owe him a favor. I kinda thought I repaid him by nominating him for the Council, but..."

The sigh coming from Bernadette's throat sounded like her soul was escaping. So maybe she would judge the shit out of me for making that deal. Super.

"You made a deal with a demon for a favor of his choosing, and because you gave him what he wanted without him having to ask for it, he essentially gets a freebie," she said, finishing my sentence.

"Pretty much."

"Didn't anyone ever tell you not to make deals with demons?" She said it like only an airheaded infant with no common sense could ever possibly *not* know this. To her credit, it should be a "no shit" kind of response, but being a Rogue for as long as I was, those little tidbits of wisdom were hard to come by.

"Since I didn't even know demons existed until a year ago, that would be a hard no."

Not that it took a genius to put it together, though.

Bernadette's visage flickered again, and the gravity of my particular predicament settled like a lead weight in my stomach.

"Making a deal with a demon is quite like making a deal with a Fae. They are concrete and binding, and there isn't a loophole big enough to wriggle through. And refusing to hold up your end of the bargain means nasty things. I hope whatever he asks of you, you can stomach."

Because I would be completing the bargain. Whether I liked it or not. *Got it.*

"Before I made it, I told him the favor couldn't include sex or murder, so at least there's that?" I said, wincing as I took another sip of my tea.

Bernadette's lips twisted like those caveats weren't enough coverage for my ass that was currently swinging in the wind.

"At least that's something. Honestly, I doubt the Council would have charged you. Not for a Quinn."

I thought back at all the times I'd been charged for something I not only didn't do but was actually executed for. *Not that those executions took...* Yeah, I highly doubted the Council would have refrained from torching me on the spot. Even if some of them were my friends.

Trying to keep my skepticism off my face, I prodded my grandmother for info.

"Tell me more about the Quinns. What am I getting myself into?"

Settling back in her chair, Bernadette began sipping her tea. Not a good sign.

"I don't know much about Alistair other than when he helped take out the Keys, but if I had to guess, he's nothing like his family. Clotho sure hates him, but she hates all the Quinns. Not just Alistair. His father is a piece of work, and from what I've heard, his mother isn't much better. If you can avoid his family while you deal with Alistair, it would be for the best."

I tried to reconcile the man who'd stood up to me and stood by me in battle, with the man the Fates and my grandmother warned me off of. The man who'd given me the best kiss I'd ever received while also not treating me like spun glass. The man who'd made me take a deal to keep my ass out of hot water, but held my hair back when I'd gotten hit with a nasty case of backlash.

It made sense, and it didn't.

Everyone said Alistair wasn't like his family—not that I knew exactly what that meant—but I could see their trepidation, too. He seemed cold and aloof when

I'd first met him, but he'd changed so much since then. I didn't know if I saw something he didn't show everyone else, or if I was making another mistake in a long line of epic blunders before him. But I couldn't help my disappointment—no matter how idiotic it might be.

"No Alistair. Got it." Was that my voice sounding that pitiful, or was I just tired? Yeah. Tired. I was totally tired.

Bernadette reached across my little side table to take my hand.

"I didn't say no Alistair. I said, avoid his family. But while I'm at it, I will say guard your heart, dear. There isn't a world or realm or dimension that will readily accept you two. Royal blood or not. So keep him around and fall in love if you must, but keep your wits. Yeah?"

That was about as much of a blessing as I was going to get. Bernadette's opinion on relationships was skewed by eons of neglect and pain. She was what I figured I would have been like had I not been forced into friendships and a makeshift ragtag bunch of family who refused to let me go.

But skewed by pain or not, her message was a hard kernel of truth I would just have to swallow.

"Yeah. Eyes open. I got it." I had a feeling keeping my eyes open wouldn't help me at all, but I was going to do it.

"Why don't you tell me about Maria?" Bernadette

said, changing the subject. "Is she showing any other symptoms? Stirring, screaming, levitating?"

What was this, *The Exorcist*? Was that what real possession was like? Was Maria going to start crawling up the walls next?

At my stunned expression, Bernadette started laughing.

"Not. Funny." I seethed, setting my teacup down so hard I nearly cracked the damn thing.

"Come on. It was a little funny," she said into her cup, smiling like the demon queen she was.

"It would only be funny if it were someone else's sister. It is not funny when it's *my* sister. And no. As of today, there has been no puking up split pea soup or her head doing a full three-sixty. She's just... sleeping. Her heart's beating, her breathing is normal, her wounds are healing."

But I left off the last bit I didn't want to say.

She's fine. She just won't wake up.

But Bernadette knew exactly what I left out. She knew because, in the short span of time we'd known each other, she'd grasped just how precious having family was to me. After four centuries without one, I refused to go back to my island existence.

"If it will make you feel better, I'll check on her. But these things take time. She nearly died. Give her body time to rest. Give her mind time to heal itself. Dying might be old hat to you, but Maria's never done it before. She doesn't know how it changes you."

My eyes stung, my lips twisting in a grimace as I tried not to let myself cry. Maria's heart had stopped. What if we were too late? What if she never woke up? Those two thoughts had swirled in my brain all week, but I refused to say them aloud.

"She's going to be fine, Max," Bernadette murmured, squeezing my hand so I'd meet her gaze. "I promise."

All I could give her was a nod, so she released me to peek in on Maria. I let her do this alone since Maria's room was already overcrowded.

Teresa and Ian had camped out in Maria's room, bickering and sniping at each other every chance they got. I tried to steer clear, hence my constant greenhouse pursuits.

Bernadette seemed exasperated when she strode out of the room moments later, giving me the knowing sidelong glance that said everything she probably couldn't say out loud because we had more than a few prying ears in this house.

"I'll come back later. Try to get them to eat and shower, will you?"

"I'll do what I can," I muttered, knowing full well I had no intention of telling my mother to do anything other than what she was already doing.

I liked my head right where it was, *thank you very much.*

But as I stared at my now-closed front door, Bernadette gone to do whatever it was Bernadette did, doubts flooded my brain all over again.

What if we were too late?

My gaze slid to Maria's closed door, Ian and Teresa's bickering only slightly muffled by the wood. I had a whole casting room downstairs with enough grimoires to sink a ship. Maybe they had something—hell, anything—that could shed some light on what was happening to Maria.

Or maybe I just needed to keep myself busy until I went into Aether in the morning.

Yeah, I wasn't kidding myself, but a look couldn't hurt, right?

I soon found myself in the windowless casting room, the planked walls welcoming me. Snapping my fingers, I lit all the candles at once. As the flames flared, I pored over the spines to see if I had anything that might help. The grimoires were titled by family name. The books likely passed along the line from mother to daughter until the line either died out or was so diluted with human genes that their power was nil.

Sullivan, Goode, Morehouse, Alden, Bishop, Farrington, Wardwell, Parker, Miller.

I had more, but those were the most prominent

witch lines. I didn't have any of the Flynn grimoires. Still, I started at some of the names I knew—the ones I was sure were members of the Arcadios coven at some point before it was disbanded. Snagging the Alden grimoire, I settled onto the chaise lounge and started reading.

When my neck started screaming in agony, and the candle's light was nearly spent, I gave up on the notion I'd find anything of value regarding my current situation. If I wanted to make a man disembowel himself or pluck out his own eyeballs, though, I had at least three different ways to do it.

And I thought I was vicious. Old-school witches made me look like a freaking saint.

If I couldn't figure out how demon possession really worked, I was going to have to finagle a workaround based on a locator spell I'd concocted. If I changed to word order, I could check on my sister, maybe?

If I could see into Maria's mind... If I could see she was in there and not the incorporeal parasite Elias summoned, then maybe I could coax her back to consciousness. Even to my tired brain that sounded like a bunch of hooey. Peeking into someone's subconscious seemed like an excellent way to find out shit I never wanted to know. Still, if it meant knowing my sister was okay, I figured I could risk it.

I selected a vial of Maria's blood from my apothecary

cabinet, the contents clotted and dried, but still effective. When Maria started staying with me, I insisted on having several vials of her blood on hand. One sure-fire way to track a witch was by her blood, and since the last time I tried to track her ass down turned into a veritable shitshow, I wasn't taking any more chances.

Fuck scrying. I had a better way to find my little sister.

Drawing a circle of salt around myself, I settled in the center, relaxing my limbs as I began the chants with a slight modification to the spell. I knew where Maria's body was. I needed to find her mind.

"Mens et animus, ut animam meam. Mentem mihi. Ostende mihi faciem eius meam." I spoke no louder than a whisper, closing my eyes so I could attempt to see inside my sister's mind.

Mind to mind, soul to soul. Show me her mind. Show me her soul.

I whispered the words until my voice became hoarse, and my ass went numb. All I saw was the blackness behind my own eyelids. I couldn't even get a glimpse of the faint glow of the candles. Opening my eyes, I checked to make sure they were all still lit. Fifteen candles stood with their flickering flames standing at attention. I closed my eyes again.

Blackness reigned. No light from the candles. Where Maria was—if she was anywhere but upstairs—was dark as pitch. Forcing more of myself into the spell, I tried to see something, anything, but I couldn't.

Something was hindering me. A barrier of some kind. I opened my eyes, and my gaze settled on the ring of white. The circle of salt... it was keeping me protected.

In a moment of complete idiocy, I kicked out my bare foot, scattering the grains and opening the circle. All at once, blackness clouded my vision, and the silence was no more.

Screaming. A woman was screaming like she was being tortured. Like everything she was and everything she would be was being ripped from her piece by piece.

What was more unsettling? That sound was *not* coming from me.

CHAPTER TWO

I let my magic fall as I dropped the link to Maria's mind. Shaking, I was barely able to stand, but I tore out of my casting room, anyway, nearly crawling up the stairs to the main level. I interrupted an epic sniping match between Ian and Teresa as I burst into Maria's room and fell to my knees at her bedside.

Grabbing her hand, I forced myself to utter the spell again. *"Mens et animus, ut animam meam. Mentem mihi. Ostende mihi faciem eius meam."*

Magical wind whipped at my hair and face, the power of the spell raking over me as I tried to see inside Maria's mind again. Darkness shrouded me. Even with my eyes open, all I saw was the pitch black of Maria's mind. And the screaming was back—louder and shriller —as if Maria herself had sat up in the bed to shriek in my ear.

I dropped Maria's hand, crab walking backward as I scrambled away. My shoulder hit the doorframe as I scooted back into the hall, my back met drywall.

Then Teresa was in my line of sight, her fingertips wiping away wetness from my face, her voice calm and soothing. Teresa had never really been a mother to me—not like she'd been to Maria—so I nearly flinched at the kindness.

"Maxima, baby, I need you to come back to me. Look at me, child. Breathe with me," she coaxed, and I tried to do what she asked.

I held my breath at her count of four and then released it. In and out, over and over again.

"There we go. That's better. Can you tell me what just happened?" she cooed, and now that I wasn't about to hyperventilate and pass out, it took less than a second to notice the crowd of people in my hall.

Aiden and Striker were back from their perimeter run. Della looked like I'd just woken her from a hundred-year nap. Given that it was day and she was a vampire, the fact that she was even awake was no small feat. But it was Ian who snagged my focus. His eyes were wild like he was either going to rip the room apart or maybe the entire house. All of them waited on bated breath for me to tell them what I'd seen, but all I could do was shake my head.

I didn't mean no, it was more like I didn't know what to say.

"Darkness and screaming. That's all that's there." My lips trembled as I tried to get myself together enough to elaborate. "I did a spell to try to look into Maria's mind. To see if the exorcism worked."

Teresa's gaze sharpened, and I realized she'd thought to do the same thing I did but hadn't worked up enough courage to actually do it.

"All there is, is blackness and screaming. A blackness so dark there is nothing... Nothing but the wails of someone being tortured. I don't... I don't know what to do."

Teresa settled back onto her heels, her mask of calm slipping.

"I don't know if there is anything to do. Maybe she's healing. Maybe she's trapped. If we try to wake her, we could fracture her mind." Teresa's calm slipped even further, and a wash of grief clouded her face.

Elias did this to her. He took everything that was my sister and stuffed her into that pit of nothingness and screams. He stole from us—stole *her* from us. Flames of rage scorched through me, and my tears dried up.

"I can't wait until tomorrow. I'll purge every single thing Elias knows. I'll find out exactly what he did to Maria." I seethed, meeting my mother's gaze. "By any means necessary."

Spurred on by the single-minded focus of cracking Elias' mind open like a fucking walnut, I snagged Alistair's gifted leathers from the coffee table and got dressed.

I was in the middle of strapping my athames into the likely specialty-made sheathes that came with Alistair's leathers when Della burst through my door. Brandishing a phone like a weapon, she waved it at me, her face paler than her usual vampire pallor.

I knew, without a doubt in my mind, I wanted nothing to do with whoever was on the other end.

With a grimace, I snatched the phone from her when she impatiently waved it in my face.

"Hello?"

"Max, doll, I'm going to need you to come into Aether." Barrett's crisp English trill came through the other line. His voice was thready like he was trying very hard not to freak the fuck out.

Again, I was one hundred percent positive I did not want to hear whatever it was that had him in a tizzy.

Not. At. All.

"I'm already headed your way. What's up?" Because there had to be something. There was no way he'd insist on ruining my downtime unless it was of the utmost importance. Hell, he was the one who suggested I take time off in the first place.

"Elias is gone."

Uh, say what now?

I was pretty sure Barrett could feel my glare from across town. I said nothing, but I got a whole lot of explaining, anyway.

"He was heavily guarded in a null room. There should be no way he could get out, but it looks like a guard is dead, and he's…" Barrett trailed off.

My first thought was of the shifter named MacCallan, who treated me decently when I'd been remanded to those same cells.

"Which guard?"

"What? That's what you're going to ask? Not how the fuck did this happen, not what we're doing to stop it? No. You ask which guard."

Barrett sounded hysterical, which was not his norm. Marcus must not have been close by. But still, a twelve-hundred-year-old witch should be able to keep his cool —or at least one would think.

"I know how it happened. You have a mole in the Council with access to the holding cells. I know what we're going to do because it'll be me that finds the fucker. And I want to know which guard died because I made a friend in that filthy holding cell, and I want to make sure it's not him. Which. Guard?"

"Cyrano." Barrett offered up the name like it hurt him to do it. He must have known the person. The name wasn't familiar to me, but it didn't matter. That guard was killed so someone could free Elias, and I was going to find them and string them up on a pike if I had to.

"I'm on my way. Keep the area clear for me, will you?"

"I'll do what I can," he muttered and then hung up.

Barrett seemed like he was leaving a lot out, but no one had time for me to drag it out of him. My questions would just have to wait.

When the four of us—myself, Della, Striker, and Aidan—arrived at Aether, it was evident something was amiss. The dilapidated warehouse looked the same from the outside—except for the gaping hole in the side of the building that appeared as though a giant had taken a can opener to it. Inside was dead silent. I'd never been to Aether without witnessing at least two orgies going on in the shadows—or in the wide-open dance floor to be honest—so the silence was more than a little jarring. Especially when all the patrons were where they usually were. The problem was, not a single one of them were alive.

Whoever had broken Elias out, did more than just kill a guard. He or she had slaughtered dozens if not hundreds of Aether patrons in the prison break. Men and women milled around the bodies, stepping through blood and viscera, tainting the crime scene like idiots.

White-hot rage shot through me. Elias had taken so much from me—so much from all these people—and there was nothing I could do to exact justice for all the lives he'd taken. But I *could* find him.

I shot a look at Striker and gave him a pleading expression. After a century, he knew exactly what I wanted. He did that weird boy whistle thing where they put two fingers in their mouths and magically make a sound that could shatter glass. Because this wasn't our first rodeo, I had the good sense to cover my ears first. Della and Aidan saw my motion and followed suit.

The rest of the room and their likely preternatural hearing weren't so lucky.

"Now that I have your attention, I want to know what you're doing here, why you all are contaminating my crime scene, and why there isn't a Council member in the middle of you idiots flicking you in the face for tramping through dead bodies? Do none of you have any respect?"

A tiny, pink-haired witch stomped over to me. Dressed in a belted floral dress and bare bloody feet, I tried to figure out why anyone would walk around a room like this without shoes on.

"We're looking for survivors, you heartless cow. Who in the Fates do you think you are?"

I blinked at the woman, properly chastised. I had to give her credit where it was due. I did sound heartless, and looking for survivors was a good reason to be stomping all over creation in an effort to save lives.

Too bad I had to inform her there weren't any lives to save. I took another sweep of the room to be sure.

"I don't mean to sound heartless, but there aren't any. Can't you feel that they're gone?"

I shot a look at Aidan and Della, my eyebrows raised for confirmation that what I sensed in the room was legit. There were no auras, no magic in the room outside of the people searching. There were just dead bodies and blood. Even the blood wasn't right. Like someone stole all the magic in the room and... ate it? That probably wasn't the right word, but my brain was stuck on it for some reason.

Aidan shook his head, confirming my suspicion that there was nothing. Della's nostrils fluttered for a few seconds as she scented the room, likely having trouble with all the blood stinking up the place.

"I'm not sure, but I don't think there is anyone alive in here that isn't standing. But there are so many scents I can't tell for sure, and the blood smells wrong," Della said, her Frenchy accent curling around the harsh words.

Turning back to the witch, I tried to soften my tone. I was never good at the hard-ass role, and I sure as shit wasn't going to start now just because I was some supposed leader.

"We'll help you look but clear your people out. If someone is alive, we'll find them."

The witch brushed a tear off her face, smearing blood

on her cheek. She nodded at us and yelled at the room to clear out. Only then did I glance at Striker.

A year ago, we'd been under the impression Strike was an empath, a witch who couldn't cast but could feel the emotions of others. That impression quickly crumbled to dust when an Incubus came into our lives. Now we knew Striker was part angel, part something else, and everything he thought about himself was a big ball of bullshit. But that didn't stop those empath abilities, no matter how good he was at hiding them.

"You need to step out?" I asked under my breath, trying not to be an asshole. Not everyone needed their business broadcasted to a room full of Ethereals.

He was pale under his usual golden skin, his shoulder-length hair was pulled back in a queue. A wavy blond tendril that had fallen out of the elastic was shivering with whatever emotion he was picking up in the room. It was safe to say that Striker was in no way okay, and he most definitely needed to step out.

Was he gonna? Doubtful.

"No." The growled word sounded like it was dragged from him kicking and screaming.

Okey-dokey.

I sent a silent prayer to the Fates that Striker wouldn't lose his fucking mind in front of all these people. Not that I'd be embarrassed, but more so that *he* might. Striker was never fond of his empathetic abilities.

Over the course of a century, I'd seen him shun them more than once. He purposely guarded himself against outside emotions on a daily basis.

I had to keep control of my own emotions. I didn't know what I'd do if I had to share an entire roomful of feelings at once.

But it turned out I had plenty of reasons to worry. I felt the frisson of Striker's change the second before it happened. I could almost feel Striker's scales erupt from his fingers, sense the exact rip of his skin when his lizardy-yet-feathery wings erupted from his back.

I should have been paying attention to my surroundings and not Striker. Maybe then I would have seen the Incubus step into the room.

Maybe then I would have been able to stop Striker before he did something stupid.

But then again, maybe not.

CHAPTER THREE

Striker's growl seemed to shake the room, and I couldn't figure out what had him so upset until I saw the dark-haired, red-eyed man emerge from the shadows. He looked nothing like the other Incubus I'd encountered. For one, he was skin and bone, like he hadn't had a meal in ages. The other, in no way did he seem like the kind of guy who would hurt a fly.

But Striker didn't seem to give a single shit about the man's appearance. He was an incubus—the same species of Ethereal who'd taken Melody from him.

Melody. Fates, that name still hurt to think of. It didn't make sense what we sacrificed for a girl we barely knew, but then again, it did. A pregnant woman had come into our shop with no way to help herself, no way out of the death sentence thrust upon her by loving the wrong man. Who *wouldn't* want to help someone like that? No one I wanted to know, that's who.

I never expected Striker to fall in love so fast and so hard. I didn't think Striker did, either.

We failed Melody. We failed her parents. We failed her son. We might have killed the man responsible, but I didn't think either of us had ever forgiven ourselves.

So, I *might* have hesitated a second too long, stunned by the sheer terror those red eyes caused.

"You." Striker snarled the single word echoing through the wide-open space like an accusation.

The man—no, he couldn't be classified as a man. The boy held up his hands like he was warding Striker off.

"I—I mean no harm, Mr. Voss. I swear."

At the use of his surname, Striker hesitated. The kid knew of him somehow. That little bit of hesitation allowed me to get in between them, snapping my fingers to transport myself within the room rather than walk over the corpses.

My gaze locked with Striker's, I stared at those glowing golden orbs. Phased, the pupil had elongated into a slit like a lizard. *Or a dragon's...* The thought pinged around my brain as I tried to make sure Striker wouldn't kill someone in the middle of all this death.

"He's a kid, Striker. Back off."

The muscle under Striker's left eye twitched, but he didn't move.

"Don't make me make you. Take a walk."

The sound coming from Striker's throat was like one of the dinosaurs from *Jurassic Park*.

Oh, fuck no.

"Don't you growl at me, Striker Voss, or I will turn you into a eunuch and sell your dick on eBay."

"Please don't make him go," the kid pleaded as he grabbed my arm. "I've come all this way to find him."

I did my best not to shake him off, but I didn't like to be touched on my best days and certainly not by an Incubus. Calmly—or as calmly as I was able—I removed the hand from my arm and took a step back. A sheepish look came over the kid's face, and his red gaze fell to the floor.

"I know your story. I know what the presence of my kind does. I'm not like them. Most of us aren't like them. Do you know what my parents do for a living? They're sex therapists." The kid blushed so hard his cheeks nearly matched his eyes. "They help couples fix their... *issues.* Most incubi never harm a single human. The men who hurt that woman? They are the scum of our kind, the scum of all Ethereals. *Please...*"

Incubi were said to feed off the sexual energy of others. If this kid was skin and bone, that meant he hadn't fed in some time—if at all, given his age, which I pegged at no more than sixteen. It would make sense to see an incubus in a club like this where sex was happening literally everywhere. But if he came today of all days, he might have seen something.

"What's your name, kid, and what in the Fates are you doing here of all places?"

"Keane, Highness. And I am here to ask for Striker's help."

The "highness" threw me a little, but the need for Striker's help threw me a whole lot more.

I turned back to Striker, my eyebrow raised, and he growled again before rolling his eyes. The action was more than a little unsettling. The scales receded from Striker's skin, and bit by bit, his wings folded back into his body. His shirt was toast, but he was calmer and less murdery.

Maybe.

"What could you ever ask of me that I would give you? Knowing what you know, how could you think I'd give you anything?"

"I don't know if now is the time," the kid—Keane—hedged, his gaze sweeping the death and destruction of the decimated Witch club. "You're needed here, and maybe... maybe what happened is for the best. I—I don't know what to do. I don't know what's best."

This kid had a point, but I still wanted to know what he needed so bad that he'd ask the man with the biggest grudge, and who was the least likely to help him. But the smell of blood was cloying in my nose and other scents as well.

"Will it keep?" I asked.

Keane's attention was yanked from the room around us and back to me. He seemed to debate the notion for about a millisecond, before nodding. "I—I think so?"

I decided clarification was my best course of action.

"Will someone die because you waited? Will someone be lost forever? Will the world as you know it change for the worse because you didn't tell us right now?"

He lifted a skinny arm and waggled his hand at me.

"Okay, here's what we're gonna do. You're going to talk to this nice lady and tell her what is going on." I gestured to Della, who gave him a classy little wave. "No compulsion, no persuasion, no using your abilities. Just tell her straight up. If she thinks it is actionable, we'll see, okay? If not..." I trailed off as I gestured around the room. "It'll have to wait. Okay?"

Keane nodded vigorously, seeming glad he didn't have to talk to Striker anymore.

I pulled Della aside for a moment to make sure she knew to ask if he'd seen anything here while he was spilling his guts to her. I left it with a warning, but all I got was sass.

"He's an incubus. Be careful," I informed her, only to get rolled eyes in return.

"Only you two couldn't spot an incubus at fifty paces. Every other Ethereal knows what to look for. Plus, he can't get inside here." She tapped her temple as she swept Keane away from the wreckage of the room.

Fair enough.

One problem down. I gave Aidan the high sign, and not a moment later, he materialized himself right next to us.

"Go through the room. Consume any that you need to. Call in backup if you need it. Call Aurelia and get some phoenixes here. Knowing her, some are probably already headed this way, but this place is warded out the ass, so I don't want to assume. We're going to find Barrett and inspect Elias's cell. Call me if you run into any trouble. Cool?"

Aidan searched the room, not even a stitch of hunger on his face amid all this death.

"Anything else you want me to tackle?" he asked. "Maybe I should get on that whole world peace thing while I'm at it."

My eye started twitching, and it took all the meager decorum I possessed not to junk-punch him on the spot. I settled for stating the obvious.

"Barrett called me for help, but he's nowhere to be found even in the middle of this clusterfuck. This means something is holding him up, and that something is probably not good if a twelve-hundred-year-old witch can't handle it. Out of the two of us, I undoubtedly have the worst job, so when you decide to sack up, please let me know."

Aidan pursed his lips as he fished his phone from his leathers. "I'll call Aurelia."

"Aces," I muttered and pivoted toward the hallway that housed the high courtroom, dragging Striker behind me as I went.

The magic in the corridor felt off, like a spell was still in the middle of its cycle. I could feel the motes of it against my skin. All of a sudden, Striker let out a guttural moan. It was pained like something was being ripped from him.

A flash of red snagged my gaze, and I whipped my head toward him. His scales were back, his pupils slit like a cat's, and then his wings erupted from his back.

"Strike?" I hedged, backing away—not that I could go anywhere in this suddenly tiny space.

"Something... wrong... can't... control phase," he grunted as he crouched on the stone floor. His body whipped, his wings shivering as magic buffeted him.

Fangs I never knew he had, grew from his mouth as talons erupted from his fingers. Scales crept up his neck as his eyes glowed gold.

What. The. Fuck.

I debated a break spell for about a second before I cast it. Blowing on my fingers, I muttered the break spell as I spun the working breath on the pads of them, the spell strengthening with every widdershins—or counter-clockwise—revolution.

Undoing, unraveling.

Subsisto, tardo, confuto, concesso, subflamino, insisto, conquiesco, finis…

But my spell didn't seem to have enough juice, and while it looked to be staving off any further phasing—turning Striker into… *I have no idea what*—it wasn't stopping him from advancing on me. Rising from his crouch, Striker took a single stuttered step and then another.

Through his fangs, he growled a single word: "Run." And so, I did, I ran directly for the high courtroom and threw the door open…

Only to see Barrett cowering against the dais with a phased and feral Marcus pinning him in.

Fuck.

The spell I'd felt against my skin, it must have affected the shifters. Made them feral. The club wasn't attacked by one lone witch… No, if I had to guess, that spell turned every shifter into a ravenous beast. And now Barrett and I were in a room with two of them… Ones we really didn't want to kill.

If I couldn't stop Striker—who was maybe half Marcus' age—there was absolutely no way I was going to be able to stop the Alpha without some serious reper-cussions.

You know, like death.

Watching as saliva dripped from Marcus' fangs, I begged the universe not to make me kill my friends—my family.

I tore my rapt attention off Marcus and met Barrett's gaze. He appeared unmauled, but he was holding his right arm funny as if the limb was dislocated.

"Ch-channel me. The spell is too strong," he stuttered—likely going into shock if his pale, sweaty skin was anything to go by.

I couldn't channel Barrett from this far away, though. Then he did something I didn't expect. He pulled an athame from his belt and sliced open the top of his forearm before tossing me the blade.

Somehow, I snatched the knife midair, wiping the blood on my palms as I gathered the ambient magic in the air. I opened my arms wide and then brought my hands together in a resounding crack, performing the only other spell that I knew worked on shifters.

"*Ipsum revelare*," I shouted into the cavernous room, praying to the Fates that this bit of magic turned my usually level-headed friends back to themselves.

Striker's guttural sounds of agony mirrored Marcus' howl of rage. The pair lunged for me but fell several feet short when their phases hit them. Bones snapped in Striker's case, and Marcus' wolf body disappeared in a wave of mist, only to return in the shape of the man I knew.

Barrett slid down to his ass on the last step of the dais, his bout of shock getting the best of him. I left the knuckleheads to fend for themselves and moved to Barrett.

"What was the name of that healing spell you did on me again?" I asked, trying to make him chuckle. Barrett was an expert at several things, healing one of many. Living as long as he had, had given him all the time in the world to expand his repertoire. The one time he'd healed me was after I'd gone toe-to-toe with a prince of Hell and nearly lost, only healing my wounds after I'd broken into the high courtroom and almost killed him.

Luckily for me, Barrett was a forgiving man. He chuckled and then immediately groaned. Maybe laughing was better suited for later.

"*Sanitatem,*" Barrett muttered, hissing when I put my hand over his cut to ebb the flow of blood leaking out of him.

I muttered the word and then snapped my fingers, only to have them do nothing. Frowning, I tried again. Maybe being what I was, I couldn't perform healing spells. Perhaps I'd taken all the magic in the room, and none was left.

"I don't know what's wrong," I mumbled, trying the spell again and watching it fail.

It was a tiny healing spell. I'd moved the ground beneath my feet, rendered ancient artifacts to ash and dust.

Why couldn't I heal a simple cut?

Why did it take so much effort to stop Striker and Marcus?

Why did I have to channel Barrett at all?

And what the hell was I going to do if the magic I needed was failing me?

CHAPTER FOUR

A hand on my shoulder startled the hell out of me. Marcus stood on the bottom step of the dais, bloody and rumpled, but seemingly fine. His gaze was laser-locked on his mate as he gently moved me out of the way.

I watched him closely to see if my spell—and his mind—held up. The fact that he was in his human shape spelled good things, but I had a sneaking suspicion the attack wasn't over yet. Or maybe because my magic wasn't working correctly, it was a macabre bit of wishful thinking on my part. I really didn't like that about myself.

Marcus helped Barrett to stand, and I hastened to collect Striker, the big lug still somewhat out of it as he tried to help me help him up. It was a mess, but somehow, together, we got him upright. Even if it wasn't on his own two feet.

"We need to get out of the pall of this spell. I can't cast in here, and I'm pretty sure my ribs are busted, love," Barrett murmured, unable to make his voice rise above much more than a whisper.

"Same," I told Marcus. "It took everything I had and some of Barrett's magic to get you guys to shift back."

"We're alive, and that's all I fucking care about," Marcus muttered as he carefully guided Barrett to the door, holding his husband as if he might break in his arms. "Did you see the club?"

Solemnly, I nodded. "I had Aidan call in the phoenixes, and as soon as I inspect Elias' cell, I'll be tracking his ass down. By the way, what the fuck happened here? Was it...?" I trailed off, trying to figure out how to word what I wanted to say without casting blame. "Did all the shifters in the club get that same spell, or was it something else?"

Marcus' steps stuttered to a stop, and he leveled me with a look so searching I actually flinched at the weight of it.

"Both, Max. It was most definitely both."

Marcus led us to the door that led to the pack home. I still didn't quite know exactly where the house was located, but I figured it was rude to ask. If they wanted me to know, they would have told me by now. We paused there while Marcus put the pieces together for me.

"We noticed something amiss a few hours ago. Fights breaking out in the club, shifters and witches acting up. Usually it's all free love and excess, but it turned ugly fast. Witches tried to break up the drama only to find they couldn't cast. Then the shifters started phasing. I took one look at the room and locked Barrett and myself into the high courtroom. I thought the Fae-built door would protect us, but whatever the spell was had a way to combat Fae magic. I was sure I was going to kill my own husband until you walked in." Marcus let out a wet-sounding chuckle like he was holding back tears. "I couldn't control it. I tried so hard, but I couldn't... Thank you."

But I didn't want a thank you. I didn't want to even think of what might have happened. Marcus and Barrett had become so dear to me in such a short amount of time. I couldn't imagine my life without them, and that shot a bolt of fear through me that had more than a little staying power.

In my life, everyone left. But I didn't want to live that way anymore. I had people now. I just had to make sure they stayed alive.

"Why does the building look like a giant took a can opener to it?" Striker asked, echoing my earlier thoughts.

"Cinder," Barrett croaked. "She phased right along with everyone else. It affected anyone with another form. It turned them all."

A thought crossed my mind the same time it fell out of my mouth. "Where's the rest of the Council?"

It was bad enough we had a dragon to find. Trying to find a phased angel and demon would be so much worse. The image of Alistair's phased form flashed in my mind. I could just imagine the level of apocalypse drama that would be on the news if we had his blackened and burning form walking down Colfax. The collective internet would shit itself.

"Not here. Caim is in Brazil visiting some of his progeny, Alistair is in Hell making sure his replacement is trained, and Gorgon is doing whatever he does when he's not here. Since he's a warlock, I have absolutely no idea what that is. He tried to tell me once and I had a headache for like a week, so I don't ask him anymore. I kinda just assume he'll show up when he needs to. He's really good at that."

Knowing what I knew about Gorgon—and that wasn't much—that sounded about right.

"We should call the phoenixes off," I mused. "It's bad enough the building is ripped open. We don't need to burn the place down, too."

Then again, the spell didn't seem to be causing Aidan

to phase, so maybe it didn't affect his kind. Maybe it wouldn't affect the phoenixes, either.

Striker and I left them to their healing and relayed the unintentional shifting problem to Aidan.

He simply shrugged. "I don't choose this form or the other," he explained, "I change to eat, but I live in this form. The phoenixes, though, will turn if they came here... which is exactly what Aurelia said when I called her. She said no phoenix will come for the dead until you remove the *grigri* pouches from the ledges of every door. She said they disrupted the magics of the doors and probably Elias' cell. She said for you to study the contents of them, but not to touch. She said the rowan tree shavings would hurt you, but she didn't want to tell me why. She wants you to call her so you can discuss it. She did leave us with a big clue. Aurelia told me that none of the ingredients affected the demon patrons."

That was a lot of info to digest, but I couldn't call her. Not in the middle of all this. Before I could open my mouth to ask if he'd started removing the *grigri* pouches, Aidan cut me off. "Yes, Della is collecting the bags now. I have no idea what to do with them once we have them all, but she's getting this place back to normal so the witches can cast, and the shifters won't go bananas."

"Do we need to look for all the shifters that went gonzo?" Striker asked, taking the words right out of my mouth.

"No," I answered. "If there were any Keys left in the building, they would have gone after them. This whole thing was one big diversion. We need to find Elias. Whoever he was working for is probably a demon, and if I can turn his Ethereal side off, maybe another demon can turn it back on again. Also… there may or may not be a dragon on the loose in downtown Denver. We might need to get on that."

Aidan stuffed his hands in his pockets and pursed his lips. "What do we do with the pouches?"

Most spells needed two elements to overload and break them.

"Fire and water. Set the bags on fire, drown the embers in water. Just do it away from anyone who is affected by the ingredients. The embers may be toxic. Before you do, let me inspect one. If there is something else that can hurt me in them, I want to know what it is."

Rowan. I couldn't remember a time I'd ever been in the presence of a rowan tree. I didn't use them in any of my spells. I was tempted to research them, but now was not the time. Now was not the time to do half the shit I wanted to do.

Shaking myself out of my swirling thoughts, I caught Striker and Aidan having a full conversation with their facial expressions alone. I had a feeling it was something about me, but once again, I didn't have the time to ask.

"I need to see Elias' cell. Has Della removed that pouch?" I asked, catching the boys off guard.

"It was one of the first ones she got rid of," Aidan answered.

"Fabulous."

Now I was going to do what I started the damn day trying to do, which was to go see Elias' cell. And while I was at it, try to figure out how in the blue fuck someone planted a veritable ass load of *grigri* bags in a place as highly populated as Aether without anyone noticing.

I did *not* like this job already, and it was my first freaking day. I wondered how much of a death sentence I would get if I told the Fates to shove this job where the sun didn't shine and go back to tattooing strangers for money. Like would they try to kill me on the spot, or would it be a wanted dead or alive sort of situation?

A question of the ages.

ELIAS' CELL WAS NOTHING TO WRITE HOME about. Well, except for the dead witch with her head nearly torn off in the middle of it. The cell door was flung wide open, the nulling bars making my body ache even at twenty paces, which wasn't at all like what I felt the last time.

Last time, it had only hurt when I'd been *inside* the cell.

The locks didn't appear damaged, but I didn't relish doing a *revelare vestigium* to see who'd killed her so close to the nulling magic. If it would even work. If the witch was killed inside the cell—which the pools of blood said was likely the case—it was possible I wouldn't see anything at all.

The only clue I had was the faint smell of sulfur which *should* mean demon, but I couldn't be positive. None of this made any lick of sense.

"You got anything?" I asked Striker, at a complete loss as to what to do. The null bars were making my mind fuzzy and my whole body ache.

Striker leaned on the stone wall farthest from the spelled bars, his shirt still in tatters at his back, the lines of exhaustion clear on his face. I wasn't the only one affected by the magic-draining runes.

"If I had a guess, we're meant to chase our tails instead of doing the thing we need to do. Which, in case you forgot, is to find the bastard. I say we do that." He wasn't wrong. But Striker didn't stop there. "None of the spells affected demons. It smells like demon in here, which means we're probably looking for a demon working with Elias. We already know Elias had an accomplice. If it was a demon, I hate to say it, but Alistair might be the prime suspect. He's new to the Council, he now has access, and he's an unknown."

Everything in me charged to Alistair's defense. He

was good, I knew it in my bones. Even if those bones at present felt like someone had taken a hammer to them.

"He helped us take out Elias in the first place. Something, I might add, he didn't need to do. He didn't need to help us at all. In all likelihood, there are other demons in the Keys. One of them could have done this. Elias could have made a deal with a demon in exchange for protection. Just because Alistair is an unknown, doesn't mean anything."

The pain in my gut wrenched again as I turned to leave, unable to stand being in this room another minute. Especially if all Striker was going to do was trash Alistair. The nulling magic had never felt this bad before, and I'd spent far longer in this room than I'd care to admit.

The tell-tale trickle of my nose beginning to bleed had me quickening my pace. Before I could hit the doors back to Aether's main room, Striker was holding me upright, and I was coughing up blood.

Rowan.

Rowan shavings disrupted the magic of the doors. Of the cell. It was how Elias had gotten out in the first place.

And Aurelia was right. It was most definitely hurting me.

CHAPTER FIVE

I was getting really tired of seeing my own blood. I'd gone centuries with little to no trouble. This one? Oh, noooooo. I was either dying, bleeding all over myself, or damn near getting eviscerated every six months.

It was bullshit.

Striker hit the door out of the holding area with enough force to crack the wood. He dragged me to the right, but I had enough strength left to pull on him a bit. Okay, so it was more like a baby yanking on his mother's shirt, but whatever.

"Not to the main area. I don't want them to see me like this. Take me to Barrett."

Or at least that's what I thought I said between hacking coughs that felt like I might actually be expelling pieces of my lungs. At one point, Striker had enough of my fumbling steps and just whipped me into his arms like I weighed no more than a child and took off for the pack home's door.

Not every touch could get through the wards—fucked up *grigri* pouches or not—and I had to actually open the door. I managed to inform Striker of that *before* he was electrocuted with me in his arms. I was super proud of that because consciousness and I weren't getting along. Be it blood loss or actual dying, I wasn't quite sure, but I endeavored to keep myself awake and breathing.

I should have called Aurelia. I should have made the time. She knew things—things I probably didn't want to know. She was a wealth of knowledge I tried to never use. Maybe because I didn't want to know the truth, maybe because I couldn't handle whatever it was that she had to say. I should have hugged my grandmother harder when she left, and I shouldn't have flinched when Teresa tried to comfort me.

A wrenching agony yanked at my chest, and tears welled in my eyes. I wanted Striker to look at me. I wanted him to tell me everything was going to be okay, but I knew it wasn't.

What if rowan was like morganite to a phoenix or bixbite to a wraith? What if this little tree was how I went?

I should have kissed Alistair one more time. I should have hugged Barrett and Marcus. *I should have…*

Maria.

Her name flashed in my mind, and I opened my eyes. *Darkness and screaming.* That was all she saw, all she heard, and those could even be her screams. Maria could be in agony right now. She could be torn apart and scared.

I coughed again, but this time I refused to let a little blood stop me. I gripped Striker's shoulders hard, and I forced the pain to keep me awake. The rumble coming from his chest was slightly comforting until his bellows for help finally reached my ears. If I had to guess, he'd been screaming since we opened the door. He sounded so far away, but I knew from experience that was the blood loss talking. None of your senses seemed to work right when you didn't have enough juice to run the engine, and either sight or hearing was usually the first to go.

Cold swept over me, and a body-wracking shiver nearly made me scream in agony. This was it. I could feel it. I'd died in so many ways, but it had never felt like this. It never felt so final, so permanent.

I managed to meet Striker's gaze, and I marveled at his gold irises with their funny little lizard pupil. I was glad if I had to go, it was with someone I loved close by. Too many times it was with people who hated me or in the middle of a battle. I just wished I had the strength to tell him that I'd miss him.

But then Striker was wrenched out of my line of sight and Barrett took his place. Barrett's blue eyes glowed with his magic as they filled with tears, the cool-toned motes of his magic swirling around him as he did his best to save me. Barrett was a good friend. I didn't like that I was causing him so much pain. I didn't like that I'd be leaving them all behind.

Would they look after Maria? Would they help her after I left? I liked to think they would. I wondered what they would get up to when I wasn't causing them so much trouble.

Barrett's nose began to bleed, the slow trickle of blood snaking down his chin until a single drop dripped onto my chest. The second Barrett's blood hit me, I sucked in my first real breath since I stepped near the holding cells. Oxygen scraped at my lungs, a sweet misery of healing that had me gulping at the air like a starving woman.

Barrett's warm, healing magic blanketed me, stealing my pain. In the back of my mind, I thought I could actually feel my organs repairing themselves, the tissues knitting back together. Then the coughing was back, and I had just enough strength to turn myself over as I retched up rowan dust.

Yep, Aurelia was right. Rowan shavings were definitely on the no-go list for me.

After I expelled the last of the poison and inhaled my first real breath, I took stock of the room. It wasn't just Striker and Barrett in here with me. Oh, no. It was Marcus, his lieutenants, and their wives. Not just them, but Aidan, Della, and my mother, too.

"How long was I coughing up blood?" I croaked, frowning at the gathered mass of people.

Damn near everyone was pale as a ghost, and that probably included me since most of my blood was on the outside of my body. Yep, I was really fucking tired of seeing that.

"About half an hour. I could have sworn I told you that I did *not* want to watch you die again, Maxima," a husky female voice replied to my left, and I slowly followed the sound with my gaze.

Aurelia, along with her twin sister Mena were sitting on the far end of the same couch I'd probably ruined with my blood. The sisters were the leaders of the phoenixes, and Mena was a healer of sorts… when she wasn't electrocuting people with her bare hands. Barrett had called in the big guns.

"I think I missed some things while I was dying. You weren't lying about the rowan shavings. That most definitely hurt."

Aurelia did not appreciate my joke, but I couldn't ask what I wanted to in a room full of people. What I really wanted to ask was why the hell were they all here in the first place, but I figured that question would be rude.

But Aurelia didn't disappoint, she answered my question without me asking. Which is what I got for having a powerful psychic for a best friend.

"We're here because you were actually dying, not doing whatever bullshit your body does when you're just going dormant. If it weren't for the complete lack of wings, I would've assumed you were a phoenix ages ago. But no, you have to be a 'witch' with no coven. But you were never really that at all, were you?"

I opened my mouth to answer her not-question when she cut me off, rising from the couch to stand in front of me to address the rest of the room. It wasn't much of a height difference since my BFF was only a few inches over five feet, but her presence was formidable enough.

"I don't know what kind of fuckery is going on here, but I'm not taking it for one more second. I didn't go through my last bit of apocalypse drama just to watch you guys fuck it up now. The governing body of all Ethereals on this continent has been hamstringed because they lack our resources. Phoenixes and wraiths will be joining the Council immediately. Is that understood?"

Barrett sighed in relief as Marcus hugged him close. I didn't understand what just happened. I thought the phoenixes and wraiths were already going to be members of the Council, but the way Barrett was acting, it was like he was relieved they were taking their seats.

Maybe I'd missed more than a few things while I'd been waiting for Maria to wake up.

Aurelia plopped back down on the couch—naturally she did it in the lone vacant space in the crook of my hips without even looking. She leaned down and whispered in my ear, low enough that even those in the room with super hearing wouldn't be able to hear her.

"You and I need to have a discussion, Maxima. Someone close to the Council knows what you are, and that is not a good thing for you at all."

She rose from my ear and pierced me with a look, which morphed into one of almost horror when she caught sight of my confusion.

"Everyone knows I'm a hybrid, Ari. Literally everyone. I did a huge debutant ball and everything. You were there."

Aurelia wiped every expression from her face in an instant and gave me a stony nod, repeating her earlier proclamation. "You and I need to have a discussion, Max. A big one," she whispered. "Stay away from rowan, sweetheart."

I snorted. "I'll scratch that at the tippy top of my to-do list."

"You do that," she muttered. "Come on, Mena, we

have some news to break to our husbands and West. The lot of them will be spitting nails before the night is out."

Aurelia turned to face the room again and gave Barrett a tip of her head. I was proud that the man didn't flinch at her pale, pupilless gaze.

"Thanks for calling me. We'll be in touch."

With that, my BFF swept out of the room, leaving me with a mess of shifters and my freaked-out paladins.

Della swept through the throng and plopped on the couch in the spot Aurelia just vacated. "Come on, let's get you cleaned up. We have a witch to find, right?"

Relief raced through me. Della was nothing if not efficient, and she had just ended a mess of awkwardness with a single sentence.

AFTER I WAS MOSTLY CLEANED OF BLOOD, I followed Della back to Barrett's drawing room, which was just a fancy name for a sitting room with booze in it. Barrett and Marcus were cuddled on the no-longer-ruined couch. Aidan and Striker were squabbling with each other in a corner, and only one of Marcus' lieutenants stayed. Hideyo, the kitsune guard, was leaning against a desk, fully decked out in fighting leathers like the rest of us.

My mother had also stayed, but she was pacing the room in front of the desk, eyeing the couch I'd soiled like it had somehow offended her.

When I strode into the room, all conversation ground to a halt. So the awkwardness was here to stay. Awesome.

The silence stretched to a breaking point before my mother decided she'd had enough and rushed me, tossing her arms around my shoulders and pulling me into a bone-crushing hug.

"Don't you ever do that to me again. Fates, Maxima. There is only so much I can take."

I couldn't recall a time where my mother had ever been worried about my well-being. Literally never.

"Okay, who are you, and what have you done with my mom? You might have met her. About yay high, stern expression, crazy powerful."

"Very funny, Max. You scared the shit out of all of us."

I tossed my hands up, frustrated at the blame aimed my way. It wasn't like I was trying to kill myself.

"It wasn't like I did it on purpose. I thought the room was clear. It wasn't like I inhaled rowan shavings of my own accord. Had I known that the air was permeated with the shit, I would have steered clear."

Striker appeared at my side, his silence only slightly

creepy. "I think we're all just glad you made it, and everyone is on edge. We have a witch to find, right? Let's get on that."

I nodded, relieved someone was taking the heat off me. Striker led me to the desk where there was a scrying crystal and a world map, and I got to work narrowing down his location. Elias was still in Denver, not too far from Aether, still in the Ethereal district to be sure.

He was probably holed up in a safehouse warded out the ass. That was going to be fun to pick apart.

Once his location was found, I had the bright idea to make sure everyone was cloaked before we stomped around Denver in the middle of the day. Was it the middle of the day? Either way, hiding was a good idea— especially since no one but me could see through glamours.

Mostly, I wanted to do the spell so I could make sure my magic actually worked and I wasn't maimed for life from those fucking bags.

"I need four stones for glamours," I said to Barrett.

"Five," he replied, "Hideyo is going with you. After what just happened, you need all the help you can get, and kitsune are not affected by rowan or any other force-shift magic. Something about their trickster magic combating it on a cellular level."

Hideyo flashed me a grin that did nothing to settle the unease in my gut. His general demeanor was too close to Fae-like than I was comfortable with, but refusing the help seemed really fucking dumb at this point. I did, however, remember not to thank him. I wasn't sure if kitsune were actually Fae, but I wasn't going to chance it.

I gave him a nod and held out a hand to Barrett for the stones. Barrett slipped five onyx stones in my palm, and a quick flick of my fingers had them turned into necklaces in an instant. Each one I turned over and over into my hand while murmuring a hiding spell I'd used on several occasions. I didn't often hide myself, the obfuscation spells a bit tedious for my liking.

I passed the onyx necklaces out to the team and had Barrett test them to be sure. Each one passed muster, and I breathed a sigh of relief that my magic didn't shit the bed when I almost died. That would have been a mood killer.

Once we were ready, I pointed out the spot on the map where Elias' trail stopped. Refusing to go through Aether, I snatched Striker's hand and snapped my fingers, transporting myself to a site a block away from Elias.

As soon as my feet touched the ground, I knew our plan was toast. Della, Aidan, and Hideyo arrived just behind me and I knew they had the exact same thought, especially when Aidan had a manly man hissy fit within earshot.

Flashing blue-and-red lights colored the gray warehouses even in daytime. And the warehouse I'd last placed Elias was surrounded by Denver police.

I did not have a good feeling about this.

Nary a one.

CHAPTER SIX

I wanted to be shocked, but really? It seemed about right that the building we needed to get into was surrounded by cops. I mean, why not? We already had an entire witch club full of dead bodies, an untold number of shifters on the loose, a dragon frolicking in downtown Denver somewhere, a poisoning, and some political unrest.

Why shouldn't we need to tiptoe around a bunch of human police officers?

I snorted a little and then started giggling like I'd lost my marbles somewhere between Barrett's house and here. Maybe I had.

My giggles turned into full-out belly laughter, but unfortunately for me, my belly laughs sounded like something one would use to frighten small children. I had a legitimate witch cackle, and it was pouring like a faucet from my mouth. I managed with some difficulty to rein in my giggles, wiping tears from my eyes as I assessed the bevy of cops.

"Are you okay?" Della asked me as she wrapped a cool arm around my shoulders.

"I'm peachy, darling. I promise. This is just a comedy of errors, and I'm wrapping my mind around it."

Aidan suddenly arrived right in front of me in a swath of black smoke.

"We have a problem," he announced, like we couldn't see the big, huge, honking problem barely a block away from us.

I gestured to the squad cars. "I can see that."

Aidan rolled his eyes before leveling me with one of his patented disgruntled looks. I used to remember a time when he was nothing but smiles. Those days were long gone.

He pinched his brow and sighed. "No. We have a bigger one. I popped in to see what was going on. Those cops are here for a reason. Apparently, there is a dead body in that warehouse."

Did Elias kill someone? Or more someones?

"Elias is dead," Aidan muttered, and my whole body went cold.

I needed Elias alive. I needed him to tell me what he had done to Maria. I needed to know who Elias was working with. Who he was working for. I had too many questions, and they wouldn't be answered by a dead man.

The ground rocked beneath my feet, and I could feel clouds gathering in the sky at my rage. As relieved as I was that it seemed my magic was back in full force, I was not even a little amused at the current situation. Three deep breaths later, I was able to stop the earth from shaking. The storm clouds, though, seemed to be here to stay. Lightning streaked the sky as I looked past Aidan's bright green gaze and stomped toward the warehouse.

I felt my companions follow, and I was grateful I didn't have to say anything, didn't have to apologize for the minor earthquake and storm clouds. I didn't have much control over either, even though they were both caused by my power leaking out of the stranglehold I kept it in. A part of me wondered if I should let the deluge come if the cops would get out of the way.

Probably not.

Picking my way through the throng of police, I managed not to bump anyone. My trek ground to a halt when I caught sight of a woman being hauled out of the warehouse doors in cuffs.

It took a few seconds to place her. Her usual white-blonde hair was streaked with blood. Her tailored blouse probably used to be cream, but, it, too, was soaked in blood and viscera. Mascara streaked down her face, mingling with the scarlet splatters.

Cinder.

Her expression dazed, she mumbled in a Slavic language of some kind—maybe Russian or Czech—as a gruff-looking cop guided her through the crowd by her upper arm toward a squad car.

I wanted to be happy we didn't need to find her, but I also kind of wanted to rip her head off for killing our only lead. If this was a result of the spell cast on the shifters, I couldn't stay mad at her, but... It was a test to my rationality to keep that little nugget of info at the forefront of my mind and not snap her neck.

But I had bigger problems than an arrested Council member. I felt a wall of Striker's rage hit me like a hammer, and I knew we didn't have the luxury of dawdling.

"Stay with her," I whispered to Aidan, doing this for more than a few reasons.

One, I planned on walking in that warehouse, and I didn't need Aidan eating Elias' soul before I was ready for it. Two, Aidan was cloaked and able to travel. Walls, car doors, and cell bars didn't mean shit to him, so he was one of the few of us who could keep an eye on Cinder besides me. And three, if I kept an eye on her, I couldn't guarantee I wouldn't lose my shit and give the cops a show.

I'd have enough of a problem with that without adding my rage to the mix. I snagged Striker's wrist and hauled him at a quick clip away from the huddle of cops and into the warehouse.

The inside of the warehouse was quieter than I thought it would be. I wasn't well versed in crime scene etiquette, so pretty much all I knew came from cop shows. I always thought there would be gabbing and a bunch of people milling about. Other than a few detectives close to the body, the place was empty.

One detective was kneeling near Elias' shredded corpse, examining the scene. It was tough for me to keep my eyes on Elias' dead body. Shredded was too kind a word for what was done to him. The only way I knew it was even Elias was because his face had been spared from Cinder's talons. But he had body parts flung in an intricate circle that looked like it had been done on purpose, if not brutal.

That was if she'd done the killing in the first place. I didn't trust anything when it came to this case. Nothing was as it seemed, and I wouldn't put anything past the former witch.

Even in death.

I couldn't tell exactly how tall the kneeling detective was, but he seemed huge, if a little on the thin side. A shock of white-blond hair fell over one eye, nearly obscuring the pale blue iris, and his skin was so fair, I'd have pegged him as an albino if his eyes weren't blue. Even from so far away, I could tell they were piercing.

The other detective broke off from the scene and headed for the exit.

"Hey, Durant," the exiting cop yelled when he reached the door.

"What?" the blond replied, his attention never leaving the parts of Elias that were scattered on the dirty concrete in an ornate, if macabre circle.

"You going to head back to the station and process the crazy, or do you want me to?"

I felt as well as heard Striker's menacing growl from behind me. *Fates help us.* The last thing I needed was a pissed off Striker losing his mind on a human cop.

"I want to process her," Durant replied. "Hang out for a bit but give me the space. I need to think."

The other cop shrugged at his partner and left. As a result, Striker's rage dialed down a few notches. I had a feeling I already knew what was going on with him and Cinder, but I wasn't positive. My inkling was that Cinder was related to Striker in some way. A grandmother, an aunt, a sister.

Something.

And Striker knew it. I didn't understand why he hadn't told me yet, but that wasn't unusual. I didn't know why Striker did half of the things he did. He hoarded secrets like it was his job. To this day, I still didn't know half as much about Striker as he did about me.

"See if you can influence this guy to leave," I murmured to Striker. "I need to do a *revelare vestigium*."

Meaning, I needed Striker to use his empath abilities —the ones he pretended he didn't have, ones he'd used on me—and make this dude move on out so I could see how Elias died.

"I can't," Striker muttered back. "He's too far away. And he smells wrong. Not like a human."

Durant stood, and I was proved right. He was well over six feet and had an air of self-importance I'd only seen on nobility. Already I was not a fan, and the man hadn't even spoken to me. Still, his gaze searched the room as if he could hear us, which did *not* sit well with me.

"That's because I'm not a human. What are you four doing in my crime scene?" Durant asked, shocking the shit out of me.

Did he just hear us? No. He said *four*. Della and Hideyo were silent as the grave, no way he heard them.

He could see us.

I'd thought I was the only one who could see through glamours. Maybe he was like me. Caim said I was one of a kind, the only witch and demon hybrid in existence, but he could have been wrong.

He'd been wrong before.

"You can see through our glamours. Interesting. I thought that ability was mine alone. What's an Ethereal doing on a human police force?" I asked, neglecting his question on purpose. I couldn't say why I didn't want to answer him. Maybe it was because he was an Ethereal, and that made it my crime scene, not his. Maybe because his eyes unnerved me.

Maybe I just liked being an asshole.

"I'm not an Ethereal. And you didn't answer my question. What are you doing here?"

That didn't make even a lick of sense. If he wasn't human and he wasn't Ethereal, what the fuck was he?

"I'm Sentinel. I've been tracking this man and the dragon you just arrested. She's a Council member under a spell from the attack on Aether where he escaped. That's what I'm doing here. Now, if you aren't a human, and you aren't an Ethereal, what the fuck are you?"

Durant stepped toward us, unwilling to shout across the distance. But he didn't make it within ten feet of me before Della and Hideyo were in his way.

"Paladins. How cute." He simpered before looking past them to me. "What else is there for me to be?"

I knew the answer, but I didn't want to say it. *Fae.* I suppressed a shudder and gave him a nod. If he was a Fae, then the verbal acrobatics were about to commence. Fae were rumored to only answer questions with questions. It was enough to give anyone a headache.

"You're a Fae, then? What's a Fae doing on a human police force? And better yet, if you know that this is an Ethereal matter, why are you here at all?"

Durant shrugged his shoulders and gave me a winsome smile. "Maybe I like being here, and maybe this case interests me. Or maybe I was assigned to this case, and I'm doing my job, the same as you. Though, I might be doing a better job at mine than you are at yours. I caught my killer, now, didn't I?"

My eyes narrowed at the slight, but I didn't immediately respond. Durant was speaking in maybes and mights. That was no better than answering me with a question.

"Could you have really caught your killer if she was under the influence of a spell? If there was a death at all. Elias Flynn was a murdering witch—or at least he used to be before I took his power away. Who says someone didn't use this circle as a way to put him into a new body? Possession was a specialty of his. I should know. He tried to have my sister possessed by an incorporeal demon just last week."

Durant's pale eyebrows climbed up his forehead.

"For someone claiming Sentinel, you sure seem to fail at having yourself in order."

Another dig. I didn't think I was going to let that one go.

"Well, since I wasn't Sentinel until a few hours ago,

and I took that job from him," I said, pointing to Elias' scattered remains, "I'd say I'm not doing too horribly. Cleaning up messes and killing bad guys is a specialty of mine. Now, are you going to step aside so I can see who killed this steaming pile of rat shit, or am I going to have to get angry?"

I let just a little of my power go, loosening the reins on my rage the tiniest of bits. The earth quaked under our feet, wind whipped inside the warehouse, even with no open windows. Outside thunder cracked.

"I don't know, Princess. I think I might like to see you get a little angry."

CHAPTER SEVEN

He wanted to see angry? I could do that. After this utter and complete shitshow of a day, I had more than enough anger to spare.

"You asked for it," I muttered, using both hands to snap my fingers. At my snap, the ground opened up beneath Durant and swallowed him whole, closing over him as if he'd just disappeared into thin air.

"What did you do?" Della shouted, yanking at my arm. "Did you kill him?"

I sniffed as I inspected my manicure. My cuticles needed attention. "He has enough air to last him maybe thirty minutes. I should be done with the *revelare vestigium* by then."

If I let him out at all.

"Max. This man is a police officer. And if he's a Fae, there is no telling why he's here. He could be a royal for all we know. Having the ground swallow him whole is not the way to get on his good side."

I hated to admit it, but she was right. I had to remind myself that killing people who irritated me was bad form —especially with my new position. Kneeling at the mouth of his new home, I counted to ten and then snapped my fingers again. The earth opened over Durant but didn't spit him back out. I hadn't decided if I wanted him just walking around in my city.

Dirt-covered and pissed off, Durant eyed me from his hole. Oh, I'd made a friend already.

"You asked to see what pissed off looks like. I obliged. Now, are you going to continue irritating the fuck out of me, or will you agree to allow me into your crime scene to complete a *revelare vestigium? Please keep in mind,* my patience has already been stretched paper thin today."

I sarcastically batted my eyes at him, pasting a saccharine-sweet smile on my face. Striker always used to tell me that face was fucking frightening. It was like a murderous cheerleader on uppers. I mostly liked it because it showed all my teeth.

"Do your spell. Just let me out of this hole. Your lands have too much metal in them."

Oh, shit. I'd forgotten the Fae could be hurt by iron, and with the rebar running through the concrete, under the ground wasn't exactly his happy place. I kinda wanted to tell him I was sorry, but I knew better than to admit fault or say thank you to a Fae.

That was a good way to get in a heap of trouble.

I snapped my fingers again, and the earth spit him back out. Miraculously, Durant landed on his feet, making the inelegant task of emerging from a ten-foot hole in the ground look sophisticated.

After I looked him over to make sure I didn't cause actual physical damage, I rifled through the satchel Della prepared for me. I wasn't sure it had everything I needed for the spell considering we hadn't planned to find Elias dead, but I could probably make do with what was there. All I really needed was a candle, and a metal bowl. In a pinch, I could use some of the blood on the floor to fuel the working.

I brought my supplies to the edge of the blood circle, trying not to look too closely at the body parts scattered within it as I settled on the ground. The closer I stared at the boundary of the circle, the more I recognized runes written into the perimeter, each one painstakingly etched into the dirt with Elias' blood. And if I looked closely, they almost moved.

Fuck.

The runes were still active—the spell was still in progress.

I blew out my candle, careful not to let the smoke from it touch the boundary. If I performed any working so close to this circle, who knew what would happen. In an instant, I was on my feet and backing away.

A hand on my shoulder stopped my progress.

"What are you doing?" Striker demanded. I got it. He wanted to know what happened here. Wanted to exonerate his sister or cousin or aunt. But I couldn't help him. Not that way, anyway.

"The circle is still active," I muttered. "That's a working in progress. If I did a spell close to it, crossing it, it could disrupt that circle. It could kill us, blow the whole warehouse, or worse."

Striker gave me an incredulous look. "What's worse than killing us?"

"Blowing a hole in the dimension, opening the gates of Hell, imploding the world. I don't know what it does, but I sure as shit don't want to find out the hard way."

Durant chuckled, and my head whipped toward him of its own accord.

"You knew. What kind of prick just sits there and lets me almost kill us all?" I demanded. I really should have just left him in that hole.

"You seemed so determined to do your silly spell—who was I to tell you otherwise? There are very few things in existence that can actually kill me. No witch casting is going to do the job, *Princess*."

There was that word again. Princess. Was it just a condescending moniker like baby or sugar, or did he know who my father was? Regardless, the way Durant said it, it was most definitely an insult.

I was really starting to hate this Fae.

"It's one thing to gamble with your own life, it is quite another to endanger the people around you. How in the fuck did you ever graduate the police academy?"

"Who says I went?" Durant shrugged, shooting me an unrepentant grin.

I tried so hard not to roll my eyes, but I failed miserably and turned toward my team. Durant wasn't going to help us, so that meant I didn't need to acknowledge him anymore.

"A list of what we know. Elias is dead." I counted on one finger before continuing, "We can't see who killed him because of that fucked up working. We don't need to look for a whacked-out dragon anymore, but she's about to go to human jail. And we are no closer to finding out who broke Elias out of holding, murdered a club full of witches, and spirited a bunch of rowan-filled *grigri* bags all over the place to fuck up the Fae doors. Did I miss anything?"

I was out of fingers, and I was pretty sure I missed something.

"We still don't know what Elias did with Maria or who the traitors are in Aether. And possible shifters on the loose. Don't forget that one," Hideyo offered, the first time he'd spoken since coming into the building.

Aces.

"Any ideas how we can suss out a traitor other than rounding the whole lot of them up and questioning them one by one? Because that sounds exhausting." Yes, I was whining, but today had sucked in all the ways, and I just didn't have it in me to question literally everyone. Even with a vampire as a lie detector, that would take forever.

Maria didn't have forever.

"I could question Cinder," Della offered. "Marcus seemed cognizant of what happened while he was under the spell. She might know who cast it or have some details we missed."

I spared Durant a glance. "Are you really going to arrest Cinder? You and I both know she wasn't responsible for Elias' death."

Durant looked over his shoulder for a second as if he was checking to see if I was actually talking to him. He feigned surprise, complete with a "Who me?" expression.

This guy was doing my head in. I'd never met anyone this annoying on purpose.

"Are you sure I can't kill him?" I asked Della. "At this point, no one would really blame me. And really, no body, no crime, right? No one is going to look under three feet of concrete and rebar."

Della's deadpan expression told me she was not amused. *Fine.* I wouldn't kill him.

Yet.

I wanted to be diplomatic, but I just didn't have it in me. Instead of answering him, I just glared.

"Of course I'm going to arrest her. She was caught near a dead body covered in what we assume was his blood, mumbling in Czech. There is way too much against your councilmember to not book her."

At Durant's flippant reply, Striker seemed to have had about enough. The transformation hit him faster than it ever had, full wingspan, dragon scales, talons and all. There went another shirt.

"You will release her," Striker ordered, his mouth full of fangs and rage.

I was tempted to intervene, but really, I didn't give a shit if Striker killed the guy. I had other pressing matters to attend to. I tugged on Hideyo's sleeve.

"Can you grab Aidan? See if he got anything from Cinder while we were dealing with this guy." Please note that I said "guy," but I meant "fuck stick." Look at me being all polite and shit.

Hideyo gave me a nod and took off.

Turning my attention back to the pissing match in front of me, I waited for Striker to make a move. I had no interest in cleaning up another one of Striker's messes. I'd done too much of that over the years. If I wasn't mistaken, he was supposed to be protecting me, not duking it out with a moronic Fae. Today was just not the day for that garbage.

"I will do no such thing. Thirty cops saw us arrest her. Thirty. I'm not releasing her. Not until after she's booked, and an alibi can be produced."

Durant had a point. Thirty people were a lot to persuade. Even Della couldn't work over that many minds.

Begrudgingly, I spoke up in Durant's defense. "He's not wrong. Della can't mesmerize that many people."

Striker snarled and I scraped at the dregs of my patience.

"What did I say about snarling at me, Striker? I will sell the set on eBay," I threatened, but softened my tone to calm him down. "We'll talk to the Council. See what they can do."

Striker growled again, but I watched as his scales faded. He was listening at least.

Aidan and Hideyo picked that moment to grace us with their presence. Aidan took a big sniff, his nostrils flaring as he scented the wide-open space. I braced myself to talk down another man whose job was protecting me and not the other way around.

"There isn't a soul waiting here," he announced, and that gave me pause.

If there wasn't a soul waiting, then was Elias really

dead? Or did whoever kill him—assuming it wasn't Cinder—take the soul with them? We'd considered that a demon was the architect of all of this. But could it be something else?

"Can demons abscond with souls? Or can you just not feel him past the circle?" I asked, pinching the bridge of my nose. My brain hurt and my patience was gone. I was tired of jumping through bullshit hoops today.

"There isn't a circle in this world or the next one that would stop me from feeling the ache of a soul," Aidan replied. "Someone took it. Or he might not have had one in the first place. I've seen that a time or two, but that's rare."

So, we had a soul-stealing person who may or may not be a demon. Great.

"Fabulous. Did you get anything out of Cinder? Has the spell worn off?"

Aidan paused, eyeing Durant like he didn't want to talk in front of him.

"He can see you and hear you. Durant here is a Fae and a cop. We're working it out. Just talk."

"I don't think she's under the same spell as the rest of the shifters. She kept saying something about her son. Protecting her son. I think she killed Elias, but I don't know if it was of her own accord, or if someone made her think she had to. Either way, Cinder isn't out of the woods yet, and I'm pretty sure she just committed murder."

My feet shifted, pointing me at Striker. I balled my hand into a fist so I wouldn't slap the shit out of him. The sharp sting of betrayal cut me deep, and it had lashed me far too many times from the same person.

Striker knew everything there was to know about me. He knew every sin, every boyfriend, and every death. I told him freely because he was one of my best friends.

Because he was family.

But I wasn't family to him, now was I?

"She's your *mother*?"

CHAPTER EIGHT

Getting one look at Striker's wide-eyed, guilty expression, I really wanted to punch him right in the face. My hands practically itched in anticipation, but I took one calming breath after the other. Rage and betrayal wouldn't help me right now.

Still, I couldn't help the hurt that seeped into my tone.

"No more secrets, huh?"

That was what we'd promised each other after he hid Maria's kidnapping from me. *He'd promised.* But he'd promised me the truth before and look at where we were now. But that was drama for another time. I couldn't let myself wallow. Especially since it seemed like Striker wasn't even going to try to defend himself.

Wiping at a tear that managed to escape my lashes, I

turned back to the Fae, who didn't need to be party to our internal drama. We had enough on our plates to fix.

"Do what you have to do, Durant. We'll get someone to contact you after you process her, but I'd like to perform a *break* before you go. If she's still under the influence of a spell, there is no telling what she could do in a human jail. She ripped Aether apart like it was a tin can. I wouldn't want to be within a mile of her if she decides shifting is a good idea."

Durant contemplated my idea for a moment, his body shifting from one foot to the other as he did so as if his body was playing out his internal debate.

"I will allow you to perform a break on the dragon," he began.

I swore if there was a *but* after that statement, I was going to lose my mind.

"But, I was wondering if you happened to have a plan for what we are supposed to do with this?" Durant gestured to the macabre circle behind him.

No, I did not have a plan for that. That circle was witch business well above my paygrade. How Durant had gotten the forensic team to leave the circle as it was —the body where it was—was a mystery.

"I'll call Barrett and maybe Teresa. That mess," I said, pointing to the scattered remains, "is not in my wheelhouse."

Neglecting my cell phone, I fished a pad of paper and an ink pen out of my satchel, scribbling a note to Barrett about the shitshow we were now in. Once I was sure the message of "Get here right the fuck now" was successfully conveyed, I ripped the paper from the pad and placed the single sheet in my palm. Slapping my other hand on top of it, I twisted my hands and watched as the paper flashed out of the thin space between my palms and traveled to Barrett.

A week ago, Barrett scolded me that I relied too heavily on technology because I left a voicemail instead of doing a spell. Now, no matter where he was on the planet or what he was doing, that piece of paper would float in the air an inch in front of his face until he read it.

Let's see him bitch about not getting the message now.

Not five seconds later, my phone rang.

"Yes?" I answered, trying not to giggle. I really needed a giggle right about now, but I was pretty sure it would make Barrett rage out on me.

"Someone will be there shortly," Barrett said through what I suspected was gritted teeth. "Don't let anyone cross that circle, Max. And for the love of all that is holy, stop talking to that Fae."

"You know when you tell me not to do something, it just makes me want to do it more," I replied. I was just giving him shit, but Barrett being Barrett, didn't know that.

"His name is Rowan Marchand Durant, and he is the emissary to the Seelie Court. I specifically remember your Aurelia telling you to stay away from Rowan, darling. I think she means this one, too. Stop talking to him. Don't even look at him funny. We have enough problems without angering the Seelie Court."

I wondered if now would be the time to tell him that I may have buried him in a hole and threatened to kill him.

Nah. It could wait.

"The absolute last words I want you to say to that man is that someone will be there in less than five minutes to handle the circle. Then, I want you to get your bum back to Aether. The Fates want a word."

I wanted to stomp like a toddler and tell him no. I did not want to add a trip to the Fates on top of everything else. I might explode into a thousand pieces and actually murder one of them. Probably Atropos, if I had to guess.

But I didn't do that. Instead, I took a deep breath and muttered an insolent *"fine"* before I hung up.

I relayed the message and set off to fix Cinder before I did something stupid—like punch Striker in the dick and snap Durant's neck before he could tell on me.

I was nearly to the door before Durant finally spoke up.

"I'll be seeing you around, Princess."

I couldn't tell if that was a threat or a promise, but I kept on walking. Cinder needed me.

The scene outside the warehouse had cleared quite a bit, and only a few police officers were milling about. I did the expedient thing and snapped my fingers, arriving on the fake leather seats of Durant's squad car next to Cinder.

She couldn't see me, but her dragon senses made it so she knew I was there. To stave off an attack, I grabbed her cuffed wrist so she could see me. It took far longer than I'd have liked for my visage to register, and no amount of waiting for her to understand was going to help me.

Cinder's blunted human teeth grew into sharp points as her skin wavered between pale peaches and cream to a scaly ice blue.

I didn't have a lot of time.

The links between her cuffs snapped like dry twigs. Latching onto her other hand so I had both wrists in my grasp, I began the break, muttering the Latin as quickly as it would fall from my lips.

Subsisto, tardo, confuto, concesso, subflamino, insisto, conquiesco, finis…

The same snarl I'd heard earlier from Striker was all

the more unsettling coming from his mother. I channeled more power into the break as I gripped her tighter. But even as I concentrated, I could actually feel her body growing, changing.

Subsisto, tardo, confuto, concesso, subflamino, insisto, conquiesco, finis...

I refused to let this woman—this dragon—expose herself to the public or get herself killed by the fear of angry men. I focused all my fear, all my betrayal, all my rage at the break. Thunder rolled outside the car, and I gritted my teeth against the sheer force of the spell.

It was big, and it was buried, woven through her body, through the cells of her consciousness like a parasite. I feared Cinder was much deeper into this mess than I initially thought, but I couldn't let her stay this way. I couldn't let her keep getting used by the machinations of a psychopath.

Subsisto, tardo, confuto, concesso, subflamino, insisto, conquiesco, finis...

The trickle of my nose bleeding was unsurprising. So was the guttural snarl coming from Cinder's throat. She wasn't fighting me exactly, but my break was hurting her.

Subsisto, tardo, confuto, concesso, subflamino, insisto, conquiesco, finis...

I felt the threads of the spell under her skin pop one by

one, freeing her bit by bit as its hold loosened on her mind. Someone had been mining her for information, making her do their bidding for quite a while. Years, decades, centuries? I couldn't tell, but this working wasn't new. No, it seemed very, very old, and renewed over time.

Finally, the last string of the working popped, freeing her completely.

Cinder wilted, the fight bleeding out of her instantly as she melted onto the fake leather seat. So did I, but for a very different reason. She might be at ease, but I had a heavy dose of apprehension to deal with on top of enough exhaustion to make getting out of this car interesting.

I was contemplating just how to do that when Cinder grabbed my wrist.

"My son," she rasped, her voice thick from either emotion or from the spell, I couldn't tell which.

"Striker is safe, Cin. I can't promise he'll always be that way. He has a bad habit of getting himself into trouble, but I'll keep an eye on him even if he's determined not to let anyone in."

"You know?"

"His scales might have given it away. The bigger question is—which angel is his dad? But I'll leave it alone for now. I have bigger problems than who Striker's sperm donor is."

Cinder's eyes closed in relief. She didn't want to talk about her baby daddy, either.

"I need you to stay in this car and let Durant book you for murder. There were too many cops that saw you bloody and standing over a corpse, so..." I shrugged, letting her infer what she would about the situation. It wasn't good, I knew that much. "I'll leave it to you to make arrangements to get yourself out. Barrett is sending someone to deal with the circle Elias is in. Can you tell me anything? Do you know who did this to you?"

Her body went rigid as she pinched her eyes shut. What did she think I was going to do, force them open?

Cinder's blue eyes flashed open, and her expression turned pleading. "I don't know his name, but I do know one thing. He has spies in the Keys. Ones you didn't kill."

Tell me something I don't know.

She seemed to read that thought right off of my face.

"He is a demon. An old one. And he has ways to make you do things you never thought you'd do."

Again, it was something I figured, but her confirmation was like ice in my veins.

"I'll be careful," I assured her.

"Careful, my dear, may not be enough."

It took three tries to get out of the squad car without

breaking a window—which I was in favor of but didn't do out of respect for Barrett. Who—if he didn't send someone—would be here shortly. Tired down to my bones, I met back up with my team and waited until someone showed up. Something about that funky witch circle—or demon circle, considering the information I'd just gotten—rubbed me the wrong way.

Of course, there was no right way to rub when we were dealing with a dismembered corpse, so there was that.

A few minutes later, Barrett himself arrived on the scene. Something about seeing his freshly healed self made me want to run across the distance between us and hug the man. I definitely needed a hug after the day I'd had. Plus, there was a chance I could con him into not making me see the Fates.

But I didn't have to run to him, he came straight to me, opened his arms wide, and let me hug the shit out of him. Barrett was like a big brother or stuffy uncle. And he gave the best hugs.

"How bad is it?" he asked, but it was more a demand for information than anything else.

"Pretty bad. I'm pretty sure we're dealing with an ancient demon with enough juice to mind-control an Alpha dragon. There were enough threads of compulsion to weave a fucking dress in Cinder's mind," I murmured into his suit jacket. "But I broke them. It is someone with access to her, someone ancient, and definitely a demon. Anyone you can think of?"

Barrett's posture was so rigid he could have been a statue, but still, he managed to answer me. "A few names come to mind."

My very first thought was Andras, but I dismissed it almost as soon as it came to me. He'd been on the run for the last four hundred years. He didn't have access to Cinder until very recently.

"Not Andras," Barrett clarified, pulling back from our hug to look me in the eye. "It isn't his style."

At my dubious expression, Barrett amended his previous statement. "Okay, it's totally his style, but he didn't do it."

That, I could agree with. I gave him a big squeeze and then let him go. "Let me know if you need help, and..." I trailed off, trying to think of another way to tell Barrett about my Fae booboo.

"And what?"

I winced at his knowing tone. "I totally fucked with that Fae before you told me not to."

Barrett rolled his eyes. "Of course you did. What did you do?"

"I told him to stop pissing me off. He said he'd like to see me angry, so I showed him what angry looked like." Yes, I was hedging, but Barrett was already turning purple.

"Is he still alive?" His voice was the cold menace of a predator about to strike. I'd never actually heard that tone come out of him before, and I was not happy to be hearing it now.

"Yes, and not a single scratch on him. All I did was open up a hole underneath him and bury him alive for a few minutes."

Barrett's eyes popped open wide enough I could see white all around the irises.

Not a good sign.

Well, I thought that, until Barrett started cackling like a loon. Still, I backed up a step or five.

"Are you mad?" Why again did I feel like a child? Oh, that's right. Because Barrett was twelve hundred years old.

He wiped tears from his face as his giggles petered out. "No, Max. I am not mad. You verbally went toe-to-toe with a Fae emissary and bested him. Better, you put him in his place because he essentially asked for it. I am fucking thrilled. Rowan Durant has been a thorn in my side for the better part of a century. This is fucking priceless."

"Okay, good. He said he'd have to book Cinder because of all the witnesses, so I'm leaving you to deal with that while I go talk to Larry, Moe, and Curly."

Personally, I liked my nicknames for the Fates, but

Barrett gave me a half-censuring look before giving me another hug.

"Max? Go alone," Barrett advised. "Whatever they have to say, they want it kept to you alone."

Perfect. I so enjoyed going into the lion's den by myself.

CHAPTER NINE

Arriving back at Aether was a surreal experience. The outside of the building looked like it always did. The damage seemingly to have never existed in the first place. Everything was put back to rights, but I could feel the change in the air.

You could put the building back together, you could clean up the blood, but the lives taken today would always be lost to the people who loved them. The club was quiet when we entered, the silence deafening in a way that it hadn't been when there was at least a little hope when they were searching for survivors.

I hated so much that there weren't any.

Peeling off from the group, I went down the hidden hallway that only I seemed to be able to find without help. Striker had stayed with Cinder—hidden beneath his glamour—to make sure she stayed safe. I wanted to be mad at him, but at this point, I was just resigned. Aidan, Della, and Hideyo were off to get some food while I got to have a meeting with the Fates.

I would have much preferred a cheeseburger to talking to those three, but I knew better than to snub them. The last thing I needed was another mess to clean up. Walking down the cobwebby, unlit corridor, I steeled myself in preparation for verbal acrobatics. Honestly, I was just glad I wasn't talking to Durant anymore.

I'd take a bitchy Atropos any day of the week over that pompous prick.

This time the door opened before I could knock. Atropos waved me in like she'd been listening at the door for my footsteps. This was quite a bit different than the last time I was here. Sure, the entry chamber still looked like something out of a Grimm fairytale, but there was a fire in the grate, and I didn't have to force my way in.

I couldn't help but think it wasn't so much progress as they needed something.

"Took you long enough," Atropos grumbled.

Ah, there it was.

I really wanted to let it go, but something in me just couldn't let another magical being fuck with me today.

"Oh, I'm sorry. Were you undoing likely a century's worth of memory modification on an Alpha dragon? Or trading barbs with the emissary to the Seelie Court? Or trying to figure out who the fuck killed a shit-ton of witches in a single afternoon? All the while, trying to figure out what Elias did to Maria? And now all hope of saving her is in the toilet."

I crossed my arms and let my voice go hard.

"No. That was me working my ass off trying to figure out this web of bullshit you just let happen on your watch. What, exactly, would you say you do here? Sit on your ass, dreaming up ways to ruin my fucking day?"

Yes, the ground was quaking. Yes, the fire in the grate had spilled out into the room and up the wall. Yes, I may have overreacted to a simple snide comment.

I didn't take it back, though.

Three deep breaths. In at the count of four, out at the count of four.

The heat in the small chamber dissipated as the fire returned to its original size, and the ground quit dancing.

"Feel better?" Atropos asked, her tone utterly unbitchy for the first time probably ever as she gestured to the staircase that led to their main living space.

"Much," I replied honestly as I followed her down the stairs.

Three seats were gathered around a table this time, each chair a different yet ornate amalgamation of each sister's personality. Clotho, with her white hair and sunny disposition, sat in a baby-pink overstuffed chintz, the solid color making her hair almost glow. The center chair was empty, but I could tell it was Lachesis' without question. It was high-backed, covered in a lush forest-green velvet, and tufted with pretty brass buttons.

Atropos sat in the last chair, a seat fitting for the cutter of the thread. It was a cathedral-backed, ornately carved black monstrosity that didn't look even the least bit comfortable to sit on. However, the black made her fire-red hair pop, and really, that was probably the point.

Lachesis' absence was glaringly obvious. The only bigger tip-off that something was wrong was Atropos acting damn close to an approximation of nice.

I couldn't tell if I was about to be murdered or if they really needed something.

Clotho rose from her fluffy cloud chair as I entered the room. She greeted me like a guest, which was a far cry from the last time I was here.

"Would you like some tea or a bourbon?" she offered, and my suspicions rose.

I really wanted some bourbon in tea, but I also didn't want to be poisoned, so I declined.

"No, thank you."

As if reading my thoughts, Clotho snorted before pouring me a cup of tea and splashing a bit of bourbon in it. She passed me the teacup and gave me a censuring glare until I took it. I murmured a "thank you" and dutifully sipped the doctored concoction. The bourbon slipped down my throat like silk and warmed all the bits of me that were cold.

At my happy sigh, Clotho smiled, and that little upturn of her lips made me sad. It made me wonder if the woman who spun every thread of life got lonely. If helping create so many lives made her long for one of her own. If she desired a child or if seeing so many babies born satisfied her in a way a child of her own might never be able to.

A rueful smile crossed Clotho's face as she began to speak. "No one ever wonders those things about us. No one sees us as people. They see us as things they can't change, but my sisters and I aren't things."

I nodded before I realized that Clotho was referencing questions I had never spoken aloud. She'd either read my thoughts, or maybe her abilities made it so she knew quite a bit more than just her advertised talents.

"We've been around quite a while. Our talents grew over time. Just like yours."

I noticed she never answered the questions I mentally asked but decided not to mention it. She'd answer the questions she wanted to, and there was nothing I could do to change that. What I could do was move this bit along so I could get back to the tasks at hand.

"Barrett said you wanted to speak to me. What can I

do for you?" I asked, my tone as polite as I could make it. I was proud I didn't sound the least bit exasperated, which I so was.

"You can do the job you agreed to do and find the traitor in our midst," Atropos griped.

And there she was. I knew she couldn't stay nice for long. I sipped my tea some more so I didn't have another super-adult hissy fit.

"What exactly do you think I've been doing today, Atropos? Twiddling my thumbs?" I shot back, unable to hold in my snark.

Atropos slammed her fists on the table, rattling the teapot and our cups.

"You have been a step behind at every single turn. You need to do more. Do better. If you keep following this path, you will lose everything. We will lose everything. Can't you see that?"

Did I know that I'd been a step behind all day? Yes, I sure did. And then something dawned on me that hadn't before now. A pit in my gut opened wide as Clotho gave me a slight nod in agreement.

Lachesis saw what would be: the span of lives from birth to death. And she wasn't here. So, the demon either had Lachesis' ear, and she was on his side, or he had a way to see what she saw.

"Am I going to fight her or fight for her?" There was only so much I could do if I had to actually fight a goddess. It wasn't like I had god power in my back pocket.

"Both, but not in the way you think. Come, child," Atropos muttered, holding out her hand as she rose from the table.

I took it, thinking it was funny that a woman who looked no older than a teenager was calling me child.

Atropos led me to a hallway with three doors on the right and three doors on the left. We stopped at the middle two doors, and Atropos opened the one on the left. The room was decorated as a bedroom in what I would call earthy chic. On the four-poster bed was a dark-haired woman, shrouded in a spell of gold gossamer. I used the word "on" very loosely since it appeared as if Lachesis was floating a solid foot above the covers, her dark mass of hair pooled on the fabric.

"My sister sleeps, and we cannot get her to wake," Atropos murmured, a sadness in her voice I had not heard before. It spoke of eons of time and heartache, of death, and pain. Atropos only cared for her sisters, and half of her heart was held in a spell.

"Is that why you're breaking the rules? Talking to me when you know you shouldn't?" I asked because it seemed she could not read my thoughts when her sister could.

"Yes." She said it simply as if the world owed her one. It probably did.

"Do you mind if I take a look at her?"

What I thought I was going to be able to do, I had no idea. I broke Cinder out of her confinement, but this was a literal goddess. What the fuck did I think I was going to be able to do for her? Did I think I was just going to roll up and fix this shit like I knew what I was doing?

Because I never did. I never knew what I was capable of. I never knew what my power was going to do from one moment to the next. I pretty much guessed and hoped for the best.

Kinda like I was right now.

"Be my guest. Two ancient goddesses can't figure it out, but sure, you'll be able to fix my sister in a snap."

Somehow, Atropos' snark was a lot easier to bear than her niceties.

I stepped closer to Lachesis, the golden spell weaving into and through her, sparkling with magic I couldn't name. I didn't want to touch her, and rightly so. As soon as I did, the magic latched onto me in a spark of agony so acute I thought I might throw up.

But it took me less than a second to realize something neither of the Fates had.

Lachesis had done this to herself.

Gasping, I backed out of the room and headed back to the circular chamber, downing my now-cold bourbon-laced tea in one gulp.

"What do you mean, she did it to herself?" Clotho

demanded, anger coloring her fair features pink. She'd read my thoughts again, and she was not happy at all.

"She took herself off the board. She might have sensed that someone had infiltrated her mind, so she did the only thing she could. I don't know how to wake her up, but I do know what I need to do next."

And I did. I knew exactly what I needed to do to get a one-up on the demon who had infiltrated even this inner sanctum.

Clotho seemed to steel herself and rose to her full height, meeting her sister's gaze with her own. Willowy and pale, I never thought of Clotho as a goddess I needed to fear. Maybe it was because I'd never threatened her sister—at least not in any real way. Her pale-blue eyes seemed to burn with wrath.

"I'll get my scissors ready," Atropos quipped, her smile practically diabolical.

She'd need them.

CHAPTER TEN

The ragtag bunch of Keys in front of me looked like a hodgepodge of every kind of Ethereal there was. There were a few witches, some shifters, a fair number of angels and demons, a warlock or two, and more dragons than I knew what to do with. Each of them gathered in a loose formation as I stood at the dais with the newly formed Council behind me.

Caim sat at his usual angel seat while Cinder's chair remained empty. The phoenix seat was occupied by Aurelia, even though she wasn't the leader of the phoenixes, and next to her, Barrett sat in his appointed chair. The demon seat remained empty with Alistair still in Hell. Gorgon and Marcus seemed antsy in their chairs, but that might be because they were sitting next to the biggest wraith I'd ever had the pleasure of calling a friend.

Kyle Brennan was neither a leader nor a follower. A hybrid like myself, he chose his own path. While I wasn't exactly confused as to why his King wasn't here —he did have a newborn at home—I did wonder why West had chosen him in the first place.

I was just excited to have a wraith as powerful as Kyle in the room.

I was going to need him.

Once the last of the Keys were in position, I sent out my consciousness to get a feel for the room. I'd felt the power that had chained Cinder's mind. I would definitely know if I felt it again.

Without a word, I marched through the throng, waiting to feel that putrid bit of magic that would tell me someone had been used without their knowledge. I didn't know what it was about myself that saw the good in people, that hoped for a logical explanation for the wrongs committed, but I couldn't change it.

No matter how hard I tried.

When I came up empty, I moved to phase two of my likely idiotic plan.

"You are gathered here today because we have a traitor in our midst." Starting with a bang, I raised both hands and flicked my fingers outward, locking the entire room down. The sound of a bolt turning was audible in the space, and more than a few people flinched.

They couldn't flee, but their reaction was telling.

"We aren't leaving this room until I find every single person in league with Elias Flynn. If anyone wants to come forward, now would be the time."

Silence reigned for several seconds, and I heaved a sigh.

"The hard way it is, then," I muttered, turning to Kyle.

Kyle's nostrils fluttered as he scented the room for yummy morsels to eat. Wraiths feasted on the souls of the damned. A person who was responsible for fifty-three witch deaths seemed pretty damned to me, so I waited for him to cough up the traitor.

Kyle stood from his chair and the room got a collective gander at the new wraith councilmember. Standing at a hefty six-foot-seven, Kyle Brennan was not exactly the tallest, but he was the biggest man in the room. Kyle paced in between Keys, sniffing out the juiciest, darkest soul.

I tried not to giggle when Kyle stopped at a particularly weaselly-looking dude and sniffed his neck. Maybe it was because I knew the big brute would never hurt me, but I had a tough time holding in my mirth when I saw all six and a half feet of hungry wraith sniffing the neck of a man half his size. And his height was only compounded by the swirling black mist that shrouded his body, coal-like eyes, and razor-sharp fangs.

Here was the thing about Kyle, he might have been

half-wraith, but he was also half-witch. And witches were known for their love of fucking with the masses. *I should know.* So, when weasel-dude nearly bolted, the both of us were ready for him.

Despite the audible locking of the Fae-built door, the guy made a run for the ornately carved wood. He nearly reached it before I snapped my fingers again and the door disappeared altogether.

"So, this one?" I confirmed with Kyle before I started my interrogation. It was good to be sure before there was bloodshed. I didn't want to torture the wrong guy. What kind of message would that send?

"That one," he assured me as he nodded. "When you're done with him, pass him over. I need a snack."

Weasel-guy scrabbled at the now-empty wall where the door used to be before deciding to jump to his other form. I'd known he was a shifter, but the kind was a mystery. All I knew was he wasn't a wolf. Still, the odd-looking, medium-sized cat was hard to place at first until I pulled the name from the dregs of my *Animal Planet* days.

Lynx.

Maybe the size of a domesticated large-breed dog, the lynx prowled the room. Well, until I put a stop to that. My *ipsum revelare* was getting a workout today. The traitor seemed shocked when he fell to the floor in his human form, but anyone who'd seen my exchange with Finn was wholly unsurprised.

A few words in Latin and a snap of my fingers later, and the traitor was properly secured to the bone-white floor with invisible ropes.

"What's his name?" I asked the room. No one answered me until Marcus growled it from the dais.

"It's Embry Jacobs." The way Marcus said the name, it was as if the mere action of it was ripping him up inside. And that made sense. Marcus was the shifter Alpha, he took in all kinds, made them family. For someone to do what Embry did, it was likely breaking Marcus' heart.

Marcus rose from his seat, eyeing Embry as if he was less than dirt on his boot. "I know what you've done. I know that you have turned against your own in the service of someone meaning to do us harm."

"Shifters weren't to be harmed. He swore none of us would be hurt." Embry yelled in his own defense but damning himself in the process.

Marcus' face turned to stone, only the rage behind his eyes told the tale of a man betrayed.

"He lied. No shifters were injured, but plenty were hurt. Those were good men and women who now have the weight of death on their souls because of what you did." Marcus drew in a breath, steeling himself for what was to come next. "Embry Jacobs, I renounce you from this pack. Your name will never be spoken again by any member of the pack. Your family will forget you. Every image of you will be burned. Your children will renounce your name, striking you from every record. To the pack, you will no longer exist."

"No. I made sure none of the pack would be hurt. He swore," Embry shouted, his gaze swinging to the shifters in the front, his expression pleading for any of them to listen.

But none of them showed him even the least bit of pity. Every single one of them was betrayed today by one of their own.

"Mr. Jacobs," I said to the raving man who refused to stay still, even though he was stuck to the floor. "You have been a very naughty boy. I want to know who your boss is, and I want to know now. If I have to ask twice, I will turn you inside out piece by piece until you answer me."

Embry struggled against his invisible bonds, his weasel face screwed up in mulish defiance. What he didn't do was start talking. Too bad he didn't think of that earlier when he was trying to defend himself.

"So be it," I muttered, snapping my fingers. A fine mist of blood spattered the Keys closest to him as his left hand was turned inside out. Flayed skin and ruined bone were all that was left of the appendage.

I was a woman of my word, after all.

Embry screamed a high-pitched girly kind of scream until I silenced him with a snap of my fingers.

"Embry, Embry, Embry. Please don't make me make you. It is my least favorite thing."

I snapped my fingers again, giving Embry his voice back. "Who do you work for? Don't dawdle, my patience for fools has run rather thin today."

The whole of the Keys formation took a collective step back. Smart people. They knew what was coming as much as I did.

Embry once again refused to answer me, so I moved up his left arm, snapping my fingers once again. This time I was smart enough to silence him before the blood flew.

"Della," I addressed my wondrous vampire assistant, "please convince this man that pain is not my only alternative."

Della eyed Embry's ruined arm with revulsion. For a vampire, she didn't seem to have a taste for torture or the macabre at all. It made me wonder where all the sadistic bastards were that were portrayed in movies.

Della looked directly into Embry's wide, shock-filled eyes and asked him to stop squirming. Instantly, he quit his writhing and stood tall. I gave him his voice back and Della questioned him, the Keys and the Council witnessing every deed, every machination. How he'd worked with a demon to put the *grigri* bags at every door. How he'd nearly ripped his partner's head off with his claws, the rowan shavings in the pouches interrupting the nulling magic of the bars.

What he didn't do, even with Della's influence, was give up the name of his boss. We were going to have to get creative. If I couldn't find his boss, it was possible he didn't know his name. Just like Cinder, that information might never have been divulged. Our puppet master was covering his ass big time.

"Someone had to have made those *grigri* bags. Do you know the name of the witch who made them?" I asked, trying to find a work-around for our puppet master problem.

That's when we hit pay dirt. We now had a name and a location. Now we just had to make sure there weren't any more traitors in our midst.

I pivoted on a foot, as I addressed the rest of the Keys. "In case you weren't aware, Elias Flynn was a murderous traitor, spelling Council members, possessing witches, and participating in all manner of naughty things. That's why he was sacked as Sentinel, and I took his place. My goal of this tableau is not to frighten you or intimidate you. It is simply to seek out traitors and eliminate them."

I paused then, watching their faces as I let the silence linger. No one shifted on their feet, no one looked away. I'd have to question them all. Every single one until I was sure. I'd have to search for the threads I'd felt in Cinder because there was no way it was just Embry.

"Too many are dead today because I wasn't quick enough to eradicate this threat. Too many shifters have those deaths on their conscience. Too many families are without someone they love. So, I will turn this man inside out piece by motherfucking piece until I know everything he knows. And I will search every little bit of your minds until I'm certain I can trust you. If you don't want to stay after that, well, I won't blame you. But if you do stay, just know that we've got work to do, and I expect you to do it. Anyone got any questions?"

No one did, but I sure as hell got some answers.

CHAPTER ELEVEN

I took stock of the party raging below me from the balcony of my hotel room. If ever there was a town I liked the least, it was New Orleans. Especially in the middle of summer. After the day I'd had, there was no way I wanted to be in witch-central with a hundred percent humidity.

As a Rogue, I'd avoided all manner of witch havens for the last four centuries. Being around other witches seemed like a really good way to get killed. Or tortured. Or worse.

It would be like waving a red flag in front of a bull.

No, thank you.

Even with my Rogue status lifted, the weird honor of being the last in the line of what was considered demon royalty, and the Sentinel moniker, I didn't feel right being here. This city was a hotbed of death and power, the politics of such I had no desire to navigate. There were too many covens, too many demon aristocrats, and too many other Ethereals all fighting for the same bit of land that was no more special than the next bit.

Plus, I'd left Maria, Ian, and my mother behind, and I didn't feel right about that, either.

"Are you coming, or are you going to be mosquito dinner? We've got places to be." Aidan nagged from the ornate French doors, his shoulder resting on the door-jamb like he owned the place. I wasn't quite sure how he'd procured this hotel room at what was the definition of the last second, and I didn't want to know.

"I'm thinking it over." I snarked, staring at the street below. It wasn't a high tourist time, the summer being too warm for most people, but still, the parties raged, and the city seemed to pulse with activity.

Denver didn't feel like this. Denver didn't have this buzzing, this trill of magic on the air like a spell was being cast every minute of the day. Denver felt like peace. This place felt like I was a moment away from being burned at the stake.

"My contact is not going to wait forever, Max. Get the lead out."

He was right, but I couldn't quell the unease in my belly. Maybe it was because we were here, or perhaps it was because it was the first time I'd seen Aidan without his signature beanie.

I'd always assumed he was balding underneath, but that was not the case. The knit fabric was hiding something, however. A long, jagged scar ran from one side of his temple to the other, curving down the side of his ear and disappearing into his hair. The white of the scar tissue told of its age, and it was hard not to flinch at the sight of it. It wasn't a scar you'd get from an accident—not with wraith healing, anyway.

No, someone had done that to him on purpose.

"Did they ever pay for what they did?" I asked out of the blue, nodding toward his scar.

His expression tightened, but he answered me. "No."

"If you ever want me to make them, you let me know. Now, are you sure it's smart to go out like this? I've never wanted to be in fighting leathers more in my fucking life," I griped, gesturing at my outfit.

No offense to Aidan's judgment, but a pretty summer dress and heels seemed to be the last thing I should be wearing if I wanted to go after literally anyone. Never mind that it was a super pretty off-the-shoulder number with a flared floral skirt.

"Do you want to stick out like a sore thumb?"

To that, I gave him a scathing glance.

"I have blue hair, and I'm covered in tattoos," I retorted, my arms spread wide so he could take in all the ink. "Sticking out is my literal goal in life."

"That shit won't get you a second look in NOLA.

There are all kinds of freaks here. You've got that handy dandy 'hide me' ring and no telling how many charms that do Fates know what. Just keep your athames strapped to you, and you'll be fine."

I wanted him to be right, but I never felt like my personal style was a hindrance until I took off my fighting leathers and put on this freaking dress. Fiddling with the giant cocktail ring Bernadette had given me, I watched as the aquamarine sparkled in the low light. The beauty of the stone totally distracted the eye from the etched runes that kept me hidden.

The only thing that kept me even a little calm was the pair of athames strapped to the outside of my thighs under my skirt.

"If we didn't have to mingle with the locals, I would have advised you differently, but word on the street is that this lady is no one to mess with. If we want to find out anything, we can't come off as a threat."

It sounded like an excellent way to get my ass kicked, but whatever. I let Aidan lead the way to a little hole-in-the-wall spot named Sonny's that should be quiet but was just as crowded as every other fucking bar in this town. Della and Hideyo shadowed us, hanging back on the street as they kept an eye out for trouble. There were people drinking everywhere, yelling to be heard over what I begrudgingly admitted was fabulous music. The smell of good food practically fell out of every restaurant, and the scents of a well lived-in city chased them through the salty air.

The battered bar miraculously had a single stool open, so I snagged it before another patron could. I managed to flag down the bartender and ordered three fingers of a really expensive bourbon. I felt the evil eye from Aidan, but I chose to ignore the wraith in favor of sipping the smoky goodness. Drinking on the job wasn't precisely prudent, but I was blending, right?

"Don't give me that look," I said, not even sparing him a glance. "We're in a bar in New Orleans. Not drinking would stick out far more than sipping yummy bourbon."

"I'm going to take a lap to look for my contact. You're in charge of pumping the bartender for info. I'll meet you in the alley in ten minutes. Do try not to get into any trouble between now and then."

I tried really hard not to roll my eyes, but I didn't quite manage it. I felt more than saw Aidan leave me as I brushed my long hair off my shoulder. Wishing I had opted for an updo instead of pretty waves, I fanned myself as I sipped a bit more bourbon.

Okay, I was playing up my cleavage and essentially waving a fucking sign for the bartender to come and talk to me. He was a little too human and a lot too hipster for my taste, but he seemed to like my boobs just fine, and that was all that really mattered. Breasts seemed to have a magic of their very own, befuddling men to spill their secrets.

Within a minute, the bartender was back. Like I said, boobs were magic.

"You need anything else, *chère*? A menu? More bourbon? A tour guide?" He flirted, and I let my gaze drift over him.

He probably thought it was in admiration, but, in reality, I was cataloging everything I could about him. First off, his nametag read "Byron," but it was probably something closer to Brian. He had dark-brown hair, but I could tell it was dyed and was likely a mousey brown or dark blond. He was also older than I'd pegged, closer to mid-thirties rather than the twenty-something I'd initially thought. He was a writer or artist of some kind, and he was left-handed. Ink stained his fingertips, especially on the middle and ring finger on his left hand, as well as the heel, which was characteristic of lefties.

Byron wasn't a hundred percent human, either. He had some witch ancestry based on the energies surrounding him, but he didn't practice. He likely couldn't, his magic was so small.

I gave him my best grin, the one that probably promised hot, sweaty sex—not that he'd be getting any —and plumped up my cleavage a little as I swirled my finger over the rim of my glass.

"I'll take a little more bourbon and some guidance if you're game."

Yes, I was looking at him under my lashes while I did it, and no, I was not proud of myself.

Byron refilled my glass and then leaned on the bar, his gaze never straying to my chest, which knocked up my estimation of him a few notches.

"What do you need to know, pretty lady?" He was laying it on thick, but I'd be giving him a huge tip, so I figured we were square or would be soon.

"Do you know where a girl can get an authentic voodoo experience? Not the touristy ghost tours and stuff, but the real deal. I don't come here often, but I love getting the skinny from the locals. Can you point me in the right direction?"

Byron did not like the way this conversation was headed at all.

"A pretty lady like you don't need to be messing with that kind, *chère*. Them's a bad crowd," he warned, a little bit of an accent filtering into his words. He seemed legitimately concerned, so I raised my glass to him.

"Just the bourbon then," I said to ease his mind. Something told me I wasn't going to get much more from him, so I fished a hundred out of my pocketbook and passed it to him.

"For the booze," I murmured, giving him a wink as I got up.

Heading toward the bathrooms at the back, I gulped the rest of my glass and took a right turn toward the alley exit. The alleyway was several decibels quieter than the bar, and I would have breathed a sigh of relief if I could see Aidan. But I was alone, and I had to figure that wasn't a good thing. I knew it had been at least ten minutes, if not more since he'd left me.

My hands itched to reach for my athames, but I held back, trying not to be a paranoid wreck. This little space was too quiet, and even though the entire city seemed to scratch against my skin, I felt the slight surge of magic when someone entered the alley. Surprisingly enough, I couldn't see them, but I knew they were there.

I pretended to scratch my thigh as I reached for a blade, trying to lift my skirt as surreptitiously as possible as to not give myself away. As my hand wrapped around the swirling hilt, I caught the barest glimpse of tracery magic out of the corner of my eye. There was more than one, and Aidan was nowhere to be found.

Awesome. What exactly was the point of having paladins if they were MIA when you were about to be attacked?

I could feel them moving around me, even if the magic that cloaked them was more powerful than my sight. Realizing propriety was out the window, I reached for my other athame, springing the button that turned my dagger-sized blades into full swords.

Yes, I was in a dress and heels and a strapless motherfucking bra. No, I was not going to be taken hostage or killed because I was afraid one of my girls might deviate from her assigned seat.

Priorities.

Over the faint strains of zydeco music, I heard the whispers of a spell in a language I hated on general principle because I'd died the last time I'd heard it used. I was not a fan of French Creole, which was another knock against New Orleans.

Kicking off my heels, I realized a bit too late that I was fighting against more than just invisible men. I decided I wouldn't wait for them to attack first. Striking as fast as my bare feet would carry me, I launched myself sideways at the closest figure I could see out of the corner of my eye. My blade plunged through his body like a knife through butter, the man appearing from thin air as he lost his concentration.

Mortal wounds would do that to a guy.

Hands grabbed at my shoulders from behind, but I ducked, bumping out my hip so I could use his momentum to toss him over me. Plunging my blade into what I assumed was his middle, I tried to control my breathing so I could hear the next one. There were more than two guys in this alley, and I didn't have the luxury of waiting for them to attack.

Storm clouds grew in the night sky overhead, lightning streaking the sky as I whispered the words that had served me well all damn day.

"*Ipsum revelare*," I murmured, letting the spell carry my intentions away on the wind.

Four cloaked figures appeared out of nowhere, their spell trumped by my own. And I should have felt accomplished by that—my spell overloading a coven's worth of witches, but I didn't. No, my eyes were drawn to the fifth figure.

A woman deigned to show herself, uncloaked and unperturbed, her dark skin like silk as she nearly blended into the night. Pale pupilless eyes stared at me from a face so beautiful it nearly hurt my heart. The skull of a small animal rested at the base of her throat.

She said nothing, but she smiled at me as if I was adorable. And I was so caught by that smile that I didn't notice the white powder in her hand until it was too late.

One tiny puff of breath from her lips and I was out.

CHAPTER TWELVE

No matter how kinky you are, no one ever wants to wake up tied to a chair. That fact was no more evident than it was right then, as I struggled to free myself from a hard-backed wooden chair. Ropes bit into my wrists and ankles, the workings bound into the twine burned me as they kept me still.

Rude.

The infernal chair was in the middle of a salt circle, and that circle was in the middle of what looked like a crypt of some kind. Arched stain-glass windows glittered in the candlelight, and those candles littered every flat surface. Window ledges, steps, the floor. Stuck in nooks and crannies, their wax littered the ground with the remnants of spells long spent. Vine circlets bound with twine hung from twisted nails, bones and the detritus of life caught in their webs.

The room carried the scent of the long dead and herbs only witches used.

Since we were in New Orleans, I figured we were in one of those spooky ass above-ground cemeteries that all the tourists walked through, like being surrounded by the dead was a good thing. Like they wouldn't drag you to join them if they could.

On the other side of this circle was a wealth of power, but on my side? All I felt was the burning of the ropes.

The fact that none of my spells to free myself were working might have also contributed to my stress.

A giggle like tinkling wind chimes yanked my gaze from my infernal bonds to the beauty sitting across the room. She was sitting on an apothecary stool in front of a cabinet with more drawers and cubbies than I could count at the moment. In her hands was a bronze bowl, and she ground a pestle into the contents before setting it aside. The woman's skin was so dark that it seemed to gleam in the low light, and I realized just a bit too late that this was the same woman who knocked me out in the first place. I could have sworn she wasn't there a moment ago, and it was completely possible she wasn't.

"What was in that powder you blew at me? My brain feels like it's on fire," I groaned, trying not to insult the woman who took me out with fucking dust.

She got up from her stool, moving like water on silk,

and that was when I got the impression that this woman wasn't even in the realm of human. Not that I thought she was one before, but still. Witches walked like humans. This woman flowed like the ground moved with her and not the other way around.

She folded herself into a scarlet high-backed chintz chair that seemed to have come from nowhere. I could have sworn I remembered her eyes being pale and pupilless, but now they were a whiskey brown.

"A little bit of this and a little bit of that. I can't be spilling all my secrets before we're even introduced. I'm Deya Baptiste. A little bird told me you, Sentinel, were here in my city looking for me."

Her accent was hard to place. Maybe she'd lived so long, she didn't have one anymore. Then, her form flickered a bit. One second she was the woman sitting in the chair, and the next she was a winged monster with fangs for teeth and a permanent snarl. Then she was back again, fingering the tiny skull at her neck. Getting more than a cursory glance at it, it appeared to be a raven's. And I focused on the skull at her neck rather than my current predicament.

Denial was my friend.

Had I known Deya was more than what she was billed as—a witch practicing voodoo in New Orleans—then I might have told Aidan to shove his wardrobe advice where the sun didn't shine. But as it stood, there was no fucking way this woman was a witch. No, she was something else. Something—or someone—I didn't want to cross. I swallowed the thick trepidation in my throat and answered her.

"That's correct. I came here for you," I replied, wondering if she was a demon of some kind or something else entirely.

Deya's smile stretched wide, as if my coming here was a delight, and she was finally having a good time. It was not a comforting smile.

"What does the Sentinel want with me?" she asked, her false coyness accompanied by an innocent expression. She was just fucking with me now.

My mind cleared a bit, and I did my best not to waste that tiny morsel of clarity. "That depends on what you did to my people. Because I'm not dumb enough to think they just disappeared into thin air."

Deya swept her braids off her shoulder, her expression turning simpering. "Big talk coming from a woman tied to a chair."

I knew better than that.

"I wouldn't be tied to this chair if you didn't see me as a threat. But I'm not a kill first and ask questions later kind of girl, so... Where are my people?"

"Sleeping just like you were. They'll wake up tomorrow in your hotel room with a headache. You woke up faster than I thought you would, or you'd be with them." So she wasn't a kill first kind of girl, either. I could respect that.

"And because I intrigue you, I get to ask questions, is that right?"

The simpering smile fell away and Deya gave me a thoughtful expression. "Do you talk to my sisters like this?"

Shrugging as much as my bonds would allow, I answered, "That would depend on who your sisters are, but probably."

Deya's face transformed into a beatific sort of glee. Oh, man. I did *not* like that smile. "You know them as the Fates. The Moirai. Clotho, Lachesis, and Atropos."

I doubted she was close to her sisters, or this conversation would be going a very different way. No, if I had to guess, Deya had no idea her sisters were the ones who sent me here.

"If I remember my Greek mythology right, the Fates have a lot of sisters. Nyx was a busy little bee on the making kids front. Which one are you?"

"Well, the historians didn't give us names since there used to be a thousand of us. We are known as the Keres —goddesses of violent deaths. But there aren't that many of us left these days."

Well, at least I was right about Deya not being a witch. But if she left my team alone, then she couldn't be what the storybooks said she was—a bloodthirsty thing with no remorse.

No, she was something more than that.

"You made *grigri* bags and gave them to a shifter. Bags that hindered Fae and witch magic and turned shifters into feral beings. I want to know who asked you to make them."

I had to at least try to get the information I'd come for. If she didn't answer me, then I would just have to think of something else.

"Contrary to popular belief, but I don't actually give a shit what humans do to each other."

Sure, and she was in one of the most dangerous cities in the United States for the food. I didn't believe that for a second.

"They weren't humans. They were witches. Shifters," I countered. Not if she did that to humans it would be A-Okay, but she needed to get her story straight.

"Humans. Ethereals. You're all just monkeys with magic to me. What do I care if some idiot wants to destroy the world as you know it? Every few millennia there's something else that destroys you all. What difference does it make to me?"

"So a goddess of violent death doesn't care when people are slaughtered? I don't believe you. And there's no way that demon made you forget who he was. So, who was he?"

Because I knew it was a demon. The same one who had enslaved Cinder's mind. The same one who kept himself hidden from Embry. The same one who pulled Elias' strings. He was a heavy hitter if there ever was one, and she knew him.

Footsteps sounded from behind me, and a welcomed voice had all my muscles turning to jelly.

"Yes, Deya, do tell." Alistair drawled in that crisp British accent of his. "What demon was making deals with you in my city?"

At that point, I didn't give a shit if I owed him a favor or what he'd ask to collect. He was here for me and that's all I cared about. This was the second time Alistair Quinn had come to my rescue. I couldn't say I liked the trend, but I sure as hell didn't mind him being here.

He was dressed in my favorite outfit for him—jeans and a T-shirt—the stitching on his leather jacket familiar, reminding me of the leathers he'd given me. He'd had those leathers made—probably by the same person who created the jacket he now wore. I wondered if it had the same protection spells woven into the leather. Protection spells that had likely kept me alive while I was being poisoned by rowan.

I owed him more than a favor. Not that I'd tell him that.

Candlelight flickered off an obsidian pendant hanging from his neck. Its twin hung from my own, the pair a homing beacon for the other. When I'd chosen my jewelry for tonight, I'd forgotten about its mate, and I hadn't expected Alistair to keep the charm once its purpose had been fulfilled. But there the pendant swung, and that's how Alistair found me.

He studied the circle of salt around me for a few moments, rage igniting behind his eyes as his gaze snagged on the ropes burning my skin.

"Your city?" Deya shot back. "Why would you think this city was ever yours? And what gives you the right to come into my domain?"

Her domain? Did she mean the cemetery? Because a crypt in the middle of a cemetery totally seemed like a goddess of violent death's domain.

"You took someone that belongs to me. I want her back, Deya. Unharmed. On top of that, you actively participated in the deaths of fifty-three witches. I'm sure your sisters would love to know of your involvement. Shall I tell them?"

I was stuck on the "belongs to me" part of the conversation, so I was a little late on the uptake when Deya replied.

"Who's to say they don't already know?"

"Your sisters sent me here to find out who is behind this. Your sisters are in the middle of this. That demon has managed to tap into Lachesis' mind. That demon is actively attacking your sister as we speak. What do you have to say about that?"

Deya Baptiste was pissing me the fuck off. With my rage, I poked pin pricks through the threads of her spell. Elias Flynn couldn't hold me with the power of a hundred souls and neither would she.

The faint tremors could barely be felt at first, but they grew, sounding like a gong through the crypt. I didn't know if I was shaking just this chamber or the whole fucking city, and I didn't give that first shit.

A sliver of a crack popped free just under the circle, funneling the salt down and away, breaking Deya's circle. I pushed some more, feeling the burn of the ropes sizzle against my skin. Blood trickled from my nose as I flexed more of my power, but I wouldn't stop until I was free of those bonds. As soon as I felt the spell tear, I was up and out of my chair, wiping the blood from my face.

I was using too much magic, and in all the wrong ways, but I wasn't going to be her trophy. I wasn't going to sit idly by while she scampered off with the information we needed, either.

"I want that demon's name, and I want it now."

Thunder rumbled outside the crypt, and I could feel the electricity of the lightning racing across my flesh. The candle flames scorched higher as I took my first step outside Deya's ruined circle. And promptly wilted, Alistair catching me before I could pass out.

But while I was worried about getting out of that infernal circle, Deya had been cooking up a diversion of her very own.

Rushing to the apothecary cabinet, she snatched a bowl from the top. The bowl she was working on before I'd woken up. Whispering a spell I couldn't place, she tossed the contents at our feet. Perfumed mist rose from the ground, enveloping Alistair and I in a cloud of smoke.

And what she hit us with would change the course of everything.

CHAPTER THIRTEEN

There were a lot of things you could get away with in New Orleans. Things that could get you tossed out on the street or thrown out of clubs in most places. Stuff that could get you arrested elsewhere were simply a matter of course in the Big Easy.

Making out with a man in the back of a cab while you actively tried to remove his clothing was one of the things people just shrugged at here.

I couldn't tell you why I was making out with Alistair in the back of a taxi when we had more pressing matters to attend to—not that I could tell you what the more pressing matters even were. All I knew for certain was that I needed to put my mouth on his skin, and I didn't really care about anything else.

Okay, I cared about other things, but those things

involved more of the skin-on-skin contact and not much else.

I couldn't say why we were in a cab—neither of us needed to use conventional transportation—or why exactly I could not stop tasting that spot just underneath his jaw, but my focus was acutely concentrated on causing him to make that sound in the back of his throat. It was like silk over gravel, and it rumbled through the close confines of the cab in the very best of ways.

I felt that sound everywhere.

"You're gonna hafta gimme an address, buddy. Either that or get outta my cab," the driver griped from the front seat, and I should have felt a teensy bit of something that I was all over Alistair, but I just couldn't bring myself to give a single shit.

"Prytania and Third," Alistair rumbled, and that rumble was almost as good as his groan.

A nip from my teeth had his grip tightening on my hips, the heat from his innate demon nature warming my skin. I wanted his heat everywhere. I wanted him everywhere.

Our lips tangled, fighting for dominance as our tongues danced together, tasting each other. I couldn't remember being kissed so thoroughly in the four centuries I'd been alive. Everything in my mind, my body, wanted Alistair, and I didn't care about propriety or social convention. I didn't give a ripe shit about anything except getting his shirt off.

"Max, love, you have to wait. Just a little longer."

I may have growled at that, but soon his mouth was back on mine. I may not have gotten his shirt or jacket off, but my hands did get to explore underneath both. The delicious heat of him seeped into my palms as I ran them everywhere I could reach.

"We're here," the cabbie practically shouted at us, and I felt more than heard Alistair settle up with him.

I wasn't paying too much attention, too busy wrapping myself around Alistair like a vine to really notice. I barely caught it when we somehow got out of the cab—with me still clinging to him like a barnacle.

But I sure as shit felt it once we crossed the ward onto Alistair's property.

Lust still clawed at my insides, but I could think. *I could remember.*

I managed to pry my lips from Alistair's. I didn't want to. I wanted to taste those lips until I couldn't breathe anymore, but I did it. I couldn't make my legs unwrap themselves from his hips, nor could I manage to pry my fingers from his shoulders. The lips would just have to do.

"Deya did this to us. She spelled us." I gasped out the words, holding myself back from kissing him again.

"*Amor diebus fatalibus.* She was saying that over and

over again. I'm afraid my Latin is a little rusty. What did she do to us?" Alistair's lips brushed mine as he spoke, his steps picking up again as he carried us further into his property.

Amor diebus fatalibus meant *fated love,* but I wasn't familiar with the spell. Also, there was no fucking way I wanted to tell him what those words meant. It was embarrassing, and weird, and...

He opened the door and we were in his house, but he didn't stop at the foyer. No, he carried me up a winding staircase, the details of such I couldn't say because I could not make myself look away from him. I couldn't make myself stop brushing my lips on his or holding onto his neck for dear life.

"Tell me," he murmured. The soft rub of his lips on mine mingled with the heat of him nearly had my eyes rolling in the back of my head.

"I know what the words mean. I don't know what the spell does. Gimme your phone." If I didn't have the faculties to figure out the spell—even though I had a general gist of what it did—I would call someone who did.

Alistair gripped my hips tighter with one arm as he fished his phone out of his jacket pocket with the other. All the while, his gaze never wavered from my face, and his body never broke contact with mine. I wasn't alone at least.

It took me a few seconds to remember the number and a sight bit longer to dial it. I didn't want to look away from Alistair, but I had to. Three rings later, I got a sleepy, "What do you want?"

Barrett's accent was even crisp half-asleep.

"What does an *amor diebus fatalibus* spell do?" I asked as Alistair turned us and sat on his bed. Yes. The bed was a very good place to be.

"Wow, that's a throwback spell if I've ever heard one. No one uses it anymore. It's a fated mates spell. If you cast it on two people who aren't fated to be together, then they end up killing each other. Brutally. If they are —" He paused to yawn, but I had an idea of where this was going. "They can't pull themselves off of each other until the spell has run its course. Usually after orgasms. It's meant as a distraction, and it's very effective if cast by the right person. Why do you have Alistair's phone?"

I didn't want to say. Nor did I want to tell him I was in the fuck-like-bunnies column of that spell.

"Is there a way to null out the spell? Reverse it somehow?" I asked. Not because I wanted to. No, I wanted to rip Alistair's clothes off and taste every bit of his skin. I wanted to do every single naughty thing my mind could come up with and then check to see if he could come up with more. But even though I wanted those things, I couldn't be sure he did as well.

"Not that I know of. Max, why are you on Alistair's

phone asking me about a fated love spell?" Barrett knew the answer, I didn't know why he kept asking stupid questions.

"Look, I'm not in danger, but I got hit with some pretty potent magic. If the guys call you, I'm at Alistair's and I'm safe."

Barrett was silent for a second.

"Oh. Wow. Okay." He paused before giving me a boyish giggle. "Have fun? Use condoms?"

"Goodbye, Barrett," I said before I hung up the phone.

Somehow, I would need to explain all of this to Alistair. But how? How do you tell someone that a deity cast a love spell on you, and the only way we weren't killing each other right now was because somehow, some way, we were fated to be together?

Was that even explainable? And could I explain it when all I wanted to do was rip his clothes off with my teeth? Especially when he cupped my jaw in his hands. Fates, I loved that. That gentle hold he had on my face, the way his thumbs fit just under my chin. The way his blue eyes flickered to gold and back again.

"I heard what he said, Max," Alistair rumbled, his breath washing across my lips in the most delicious of ways. "You can stop trying to figure out a way to tell me."

I couldn't help the roll of my hips that brought a

delectable little hiss from his mouth as my center pressed at just the right spot over the fly of his jeans. The fact that I was wearing a skirt and his jeans were so easily adjusted made me marvel at the fact that we didn't end up fucking in the cab on the way here.

"At least we don't want to kill each other?" I said it like a question, but more I just wanted him to laugh. When it rumbled out of him, I felt that joy through my whole body.

"True, but... I don't want to make love to you under the guise of a spell," he admitted. Knowing how much I wanted him, he had to have been feeling the same. And still he wanted to wait—knowing it was almost like torture to do so.

And that knowledge made me want to sully the shit out of him.

Spell or not, I wanted him. Spell or not, I remembered our first kiss and how much effort it had taken to pry my hands off him then. Spell or not, he was the first man to touch me since Micah that didn't make me flinch or want to run away.

"Do you know how long it's been since I haven't flinched when a man touches me?" At the shake of Alistair's head, I answered my own question. "Almost a year. Not since Micah. I think I like your hands on me."

Micah Goode had damn near enslaved me. The things he planned for me haunted my dreams even to this day. I hadn't had a good night's sleep since the day he walked into my shop. Before him, I used to hug everyone. I used to be... someone else. Micah Goode changed me and not for the better.

I shook my head and peeled Alistair's leather jacket off his shoulders. The coat was hung up on his elbows because he still hadn't released my face from his gentle hold. Alistair's grip turned a bit firmer, wrenching my gaze back to his.

"Max, love. You don't have to do this."

I couldn't physically make myself not kiss him then, and when his hands dropped from my face to land on my hips, I took the opportunity to shove his jacket further down his arms. Step one was the jacket. Step two was get him naked.

I was super fond of step two.

"And no one's making me. You want me, though, right? You felt this before. Not from Deya's spell. On your own without all the magic, you felt like this, didn't you?"

His grip tightened on my hips, pressing me to him like he'd prefer to merge our bodies together.

"You know I did. Still do," he growled, his fangs nipping gently at my bottom lip. Those fangs spoke of how close he was to losing control. And the way his accent curled around the words released something in me that I had been holding back until now.

Hope.

A week ago, I wanted him out of my life. A week ago, I told him I wasn't a good bet—that he should pick someone else. Now, after all he'd done to find me, after all he'd done to let me be me, I couldn't keep pushing him away. I couldn't let myself shove him aside like I'd done so many others.

"Good. Get naked, Knight," I ordered, using his former title. "I have plans for this bed."

His smile was a flash of fang before my back was pressed into the fluffy down duvet, his delicious weight on me from the waist down as he tossed off his jacket. Now onto step two. My fingers curled into the hem of his T-shirt, yanking it up his torso. With a little help, it was off, and all I saw was corded muscles under skin decorated with black runes. I'd seen those runes lit up with fire when he'd been trapped in my circle, but I'd never realized they were etched into his flesh.

The pendant I'd given him swung between us and I snagged it, yanking him back down to me. Alistair got my hint because his lips were on me then, his heat seeping into my skin. His tongue tangled with mine as I reached for his belt. Together, we worked the stubborn leather free, but rather than waiting for his pants to be unzipped, I slid my hand in his jeans, the heat of him filling my hand as I gave him one slow stroke.

His growl was more feral then, and he caught my

questing hands, holding my wrists above my head in just one long-fingered hand.

"Don't jump ahead. I have plans for more than just this bed, Princess. I've had more than a week to dream up all the ways I want you. I'm not going to be satisfied with just this bed or just tonight. I have a years' worth of plans, love. Centuries, even. Maybe longer."

I felt those words everywhere, but especially in my sex. Those words alone made my center clench, aching and empty and wanting him.

Breathless already and we had barely done a thing, I replied, "So you're saying you'll be using me for the sex. I can appreciate this."

Alistair's grin was all fangs as he ran his heated hands from my wrists, down my arms, along my sides to my hips. There, I watched his muscles as he bunched my skirt in his hands until he reached the hem. Questing fingers found the lace edge of my underwear, divesting me of them slowly, carefully, dragging the lace inch by inch down my legs.

When they were free of my ankles, he kissed and nibbled his way back up my body, his fangs grazing my flesh as he went. Once he had me shaking and—*I'm not even a little ashamed to say*—begging, his fingers expertly found the tie to my dress. Within seconds I was nearly bare, save for a diabolically uncomfortable strapless bra and then that was gone, too.

Alistair's fingers traced my ink as his gaze lit me on fire. He was beautiful standing there shirtless, his open jeans and belt exposing his black boxer briefs, his runes stark against his skin. They seemed darker than any black-and-gray tattoo, the pigment part of him in a way my ink would never be.

I watched as he removed his jeans and underwear, making him just as naked as I was. Then he covered me with his body, the slide of his skin against mine causing me to lose what little bit of control I had.

I'd always needed a taker, needed someone who would let me give all the parts of myself without artifice or barriers.

And Alistair took.

He took everything I had to give him.

I just hoped I would always have something left to give.

CHAPTER FOURTEEN

I woke up to the feel of Alistair's lips on my shoulder. It wasn't the first time I'd woken up that way in the last few hours, but with the pale light seeping in from the windows, it might be my last for the day. His heat at my back was fabulous, and it took everything in me not to burrow myself against him and go back to sleep. Well, either that or turn around and have another round of mind-blowing sex.

Really, it was a toss-up.

But with the spell Deya cast on us lifted, I knew I had other problems on the horizon, and going back to bed or consuming more of Alistair's attention was not on the docket.

Not until later.

I knew at this point I probably didn't love Alistair. Fated love spell or not. But I knew enough about myself to know that I *could* love him. If he stuck around. If I let him stick around. And for right now that was enough. I wanted to see where this would go—which was more than I'd given to anyone else in a long time.

"I can feel your brain working from over here. Anything you want to share?"

His voice was rough, either from sleep or an emotion I couldn't name, and I had to smile at the sound. That sound was like coming home to a warm bed and roaring fire in winter. I couldn't explain it any better than that. It was more than comfort, more than safety. It was something else altogether, and I really, really liked it.

"No, I'm good," I murmured, unwilling to tell him just what I thought of waking up in bed with him.

"Interesting. Because I think you really like the fact that you woke up in bed with me, and you just don't want to say. If I had to guess, I think you like me and are wondering what the next step is. You're having the exact same thought I am—you just don't want to admit it."

Turning over to face him, I opened my mouth to deny it, until I took in the flicker of hope on his face.

I settled with humor because it was my default setting.

"I dislike it immensely when you're right. Can't you just let me bask in the afterglow and make me breakfast?"

"I will once you give me a kiss. Then, you need to answer your bloody phone."

"My phone?" Honestly, I'd thought I'd lost my purse —and my athames—to Deya, because after she hit me with that stupid powder, I was out of sorts until right about now. It was then that I noticed Alistair was fully clothed. Interesting.

"I just got back from getting your things. Your pocketbook and your athames were all you were missing, right?"

I checked the charms around my neck and my grandmother's ring. Nope, all there. Other than my clothes, I wasn't missing anything else. It vaguely occurred to me that Alistair found me even with my grandmother's *hide me* ring on. Somehow my magic superseded hers in the amulet I'd given him. Interesting.

"Right. How the hell did you get my stuff back? After what she hit us with, I kinda figured she wouldn't be too receptive to a kind exchange."

"She wasn't there. None of her stuff was. Not the apothecary cabinet, not the idols and candles, not the witchy woo-woo shite she had all over the walls. Nothing. All that was left was your things and the chair you were sitting in when I came to get you."

I didn't like that one bit.

"That is not comforting at all. I should check the

stuff you brought for spells. After what she did to us, I don't trust anything about that woman."

"You know she isn't a woman, right?"

"I know exactly what she is. And I know she used the *amor diebus fatalibus* to distract us. My only hope was she knew it wouldn't lead to our deaths, but there's no telling. She is not a friendly, and I'm checking every speck of my stuff to make sure she didn't put a locator spell or some other nasty on them."

Alistair dropped a kiss on my lips that lingered long enough for me to want to strip him naked and forget about this whole Deya business, but he was smart enough to break it on his own. Then he was off the bed, which I only now realized was a giant sleigh style in the middle of an opulent room. He grasped my hand and pulled me to sitting, the devilish grin that crossed his face when the sheet fell to my waist was an expression I wanted to see on him often.

I had to shake myself. Priorities, Max. Sex later.

"Clothes?" I asked, pulling the sheet back up to cover myself.

"It doesn't matter if you cover yourself or not, Princess. I know what's underneath that sheet, and it'll be burned into my brain for the rest of forever."

I felt a blush rise from my center all the way up to my face. Why, exactly, I didn't know. Maybe because all the decadent things we did to each other flashed through my mind. Maybe it was the way his mouth curled up to one side as he said those words to me. Maybe it was both.

"Clothes," I demanded.

Alistair nodded to the pile of frilly fabric that was likely my dress. Only... it was a different print. No, this wasn't mine.

At my frown, Alistair explained, "Ren procured you new clothes. He also went with me to gather your things from Deya."

"Ren got me new clothes?" I demanded because those words were not a question.

"It was in between round four and five last night that I made sure you would have something clean to wear when we finally wound down, yes. Would you have rather me go? You remember round five, don't you?"

A full-body shiver snaked through me. Oh, I remembered all right. Flashes of Alistair's body practically steaming in the shower, of our bodies wrapped around each other under the spray. I nodded, my anger fizzling out as soon as it came.

"There's underwear in that pile, isn't there?" Was that my puritanical upbringing rearing its ugly head? Maybe.

Alistair's lips quivered as he held in a laugh. Yes, I was born in the 1600s. Yes, I had issues with men who I wasn't sleeping with seeing my underwear. Sue me.

"Max, Ren is older than I am. I think he's seen ladies' undergarments before."

"Fine. But if he makes a comment about them, I'll set him on fire. Deal?"

Alistair's laugh was a thing of beauty. It smoothed his perpetual frowning brow, it stretched those beautifully full lips just so, and when he threw his head back and the laughter fell from his lips, it was just so fucking stunning to see.

"Deal. Now, as much as I would like to take you to bed and never leave, the both of us have to deal with a load of bullshit today. So get dressed and check your things. And answer your bloody phone. Your people are probably worried about you."

He dropped a kiss on my lips and left the room to let me dress. Amazingly enough, I wasn't shy about being naked in front of Alistair, but we both knew that we wouldn't be done with each other anytime soon.

I pulled on my new clothes—that I absolutely refused to believe Ren picked out for me—and brushed my teeth after finding a new toothbrush still in the packaging. There was more than just a toothbrush and toothpaste laid out for me. There was face wash, moisturizer, lip balm, and deodorant in a French boutique bag sitting on the counter of the en suite. I decided to think of these things as an awesome gesture rather than super weird. Denial was my friend.

At least the dress was similar in style to the one I'd worn last night, and the undies fit.

As put together as I could be, I felt ready to attack whatever nasty Deya attached to my stuff, but when I inspected the phone, purse, and athames, there wasn't one. I even slit the lining to the bag to make sure there wasn't a hidden *grigri* bag. I was positive that I would be able to see it if there was a spell—locator or otherwise—on them.

Interesting.

I strapped my athames to my thighs again and stuffed the pocketbook under my arm. I needed coffee, but answering my phone was priority. It had gone off roughly five times since I started my inspection. Answering it, I mentally prepared myself for an onslaught.

"Hello?"

"Thank the Fates. For the love of all that's holy, please don't do that to me again," Della whispered, relief coloring her every word.

"I didn't mean to do it to you in the first place. I got knocked for a loop. You?"

"*Sí.* We were set upon as soon as we parted. *Colpeunos per darrere.* They were silent as the grave."

While I was pissed that they hit my friends from behind, I was surprised Della couldn't hear her attackers coming. Silent as the grave. Acolytes of a goddess of violent death might just be silent as the grave.

"I'm glad you're okay. How is everyone else?"

"Aidan is furious. Hideyo is confused. I'm resigned to the fact that we are dealing with more than just wayward witches, yes?"

"Have you ever heard of a Keres?"

The line went silent for a few moments. Then Della was yelling. "You're telling me we went up against goddesses of violent deaths and lived? *Deu meu.* We need to get the hell out of this city, Maxima. Where are you?"

I was torn on answering that. While I knew that we needed to get the hell out of New Orleans, we still needed the info that Deya had. And without asking the Fates outright, I couldn't figure out another way to get it. I needed to talk to Deya. I needed to see if she meant for me and Alistair to kill each other, or if she meant something else.

And I needed that demon's freaking name.

"I'll consider leaving. I need to make a few phone calls and get some coffee. Maybe even get a beignet or two."

"You did not answer my question, Maxima. Where. Are. You?"

I debated on pissing her off more. The last thing I needed was the three of them showing up on Alistair's doorstep ready to kidnap me back to Denver. Not that Alistair would let them, but still.

"I'm safe. I'm with Alistair."

I didn't know if Della liked Alistair, but I sort of hoped she did. "The same one you summoned to a circle? Current head of the demon seat on the Council. Knight of Hell. That Alistair?"

"Do you know of another one?"

The sigh Della made was as if her soul was trying valiantly to escape from her body. "Do I need to be more worried about you than I currently am?"

I didn't know how to answer that. "No?"

"That tiny little inflection at the end is not comforting in the least. You have one hour, or I will enlist Aidan and Hideyo to help me rip this city apart looking for you. Do you understand, Maxima? I will give a kitsune and a pissed off wraith free rein on destruction. Don't test me."

She was worse than Teresa.

"Max…"

"Fine. But I'm at Prytania and Third if you need to look for me. Just give me some time. Deal?"

I would have hoped Della would be reasonable, but instead she'd hung up. I'd give her five minutes tops before she got here. That had me shoving my phone in my purse and hustling downstairs.

When I hit the landing at the top, I heard the sound

of raised voices coming from what I could only guess was the entryway. As the foyer came into view, I could see an enraged Alistair, a pissed off Ren, and a redheaded woman I'd never met.

"Get her out of here, Ren, or I swear I will see her out." Alistair fumed, his words passing through gritted teeth. I didn't think his flowery words meant anything less than pure, unadulterated violence.

The woman was refined, if a little stuffy. It couldn't be later than six in the morning, and here she was calling on a man who did not want to see her at all. But as soon as she saw me on the landing, she was skirting around Alistair and coming right for me.

If it wasn't for the saccharine-sweet smile on her face, I would have pegged her as a legit enemy. While I knew she was a demon from the energies radiating around her body, I had no idea what relationship she had with Alistair. This felt more like emotional manipulation than an all-out attack.

Still, I was ready for either.

"Maxima," the woman gushed, her crisp British accent so much like Alistair's. "I'm so happy to meet you. I can't believe Alistair hasn't introduced us. I mean, with the marriage and all, I thought you would take time out of your schedule to meet your future mother-in-law."

It was a blitz attack, reprimand, and back-handed

compliment all rolled into one. But marriage? Say what now?

I managed to skirt around the woman—no, Alistair's mother, I was guessing—refusing to let her touch me as she moved in for a hug. It was a feat on the stairs, especially since I was still processing the little marriage tidbit, and I was in heels.

I refused to give this woman my back, so I took the steps one at a time backward until I was down them and closer to Alistair.

"What in the blue fuck is this woman talking about?" I whisper-yelled at Alistair, hoping with all the little bit of hope in my heart that she was just crazy and not his actual mother.

"The arranged marriage, dear," Alistair's mother answered. "I'm so happy you two are going through with it."

What. The. Fuck.

CHAPTER FIFTEEN

In what world would anyone want me for an arranged marriage? I was the bastard daughter of the demon Andras, yes, but I was a half-breed tattooed freak with wonky magic. Esteemed breeding and poise I was not.

"Surely you knew about the arrangement, dear. It was your grandfather that made it. And honestly, if you two weren't carrying on all over town, I wouldn't be here now."

Okay, not only did I not trust this bitch, she was a condescending piece of shit in a pretty package.

"Tough to know about an arranged marriage since I was made a Rogue at fourteen, lady."

Ren stepped in front of me, arms spread wide like he expected Alistair's mother to come down from those steps and attack. His behavior was not comforting at all.

"Isolde, please see reason. You are just making it worse. Coming here barely past dawn because you want to cause a scene is not the way to make your case." Ren's tone was soothing, but it made no difference to his target. She was still smiling, but the little stretch of her lips seemed brittle and ready to crack.

But Alistair had zero compunctions about riling up his mother. In fact, he was dead set on smashing her reason for being here in a hundred bits. I could respect him for that.

"That agreement was made a millennia before I was even born, Mother, and I told you I wouldn't honor it centuries ago. As I recall, that was the reason I was banished to the boundary as a Knight instead of being brought into the family business. If you think that since I now have a higher station you can come in here and steamroll me, you have lost every last bit of your mind."

So he knew about this so-called arranged marriage and didn't tell me. I'd file that away for later. For now, I would focus on the fact that he'd already told her no—years ago if his argument was to be believed.

If it could be believed.

"I also recall that Andras murdered the last man to try and marry off his daughter without his consent. You remember him? Abaddon? Andras murdered his own father to void that damn deal, and I can guarantee if my father insists on trying to push it, this time Andras will have help."

I thought Andras murdered his father because he was killing innocents. Was that a lie or was this? The only way I'd know for sure was if Andras told me himself. Good luck on that happening.

"Don't force my hand, Mother."

Isolde feigned shock. She was a good actress, I could give her that, but I knew a bullshitter when I saw one. Plus, every time she faked an emotion, the energies around her head would turn dark. She was her very own lie detector.

"How could you threaten me? I'm your mother," she insisted, like being a parent actually meant something.

"Look, lady. I don't know what game you're trying to play, but I know your son. I know he is good and honorable and pretty much everything you are not. You are not welcome in his home, and you are not welcome in my presence. I suggest you leave and not come back until someone invites you."

Isolde took one step down the stairs and then another. Her movements were lithe and sinuous, like she was a predator stalking her prey.

Ren and Alistair were now somehow in front of me, either they were protecting Isolde from me or the other way around, I couldn't figure out which. Well, until Alistair grabbed me and yanked me behind him, herding me backward. They were definitely protecting me from her, and I couldn't figure out why.

"You think you have the right to toss me out of my son's home?" she murmured, her head cocked to the side like she thought I was precious. The gesture reminded me of Durant, and he'd had that same exact expression up until I buried him alive.

With my free hand—because my right hand was still in Alistair's grip and he wasn't letting go anytime soon —I fished an athame out of its sheathe and pressed the rune to expand the blade.

I wasn't going into this shit unarmed. No way, no how.

Isolde's advance stuttered to a stop as she eyed the blade in my hand.

"You need to leave, Mother. And don't come back. Whatever he put you up to, stop it before it gets you killed."

I wondered who *he* was. I also wondered what power his mother had that was so bad he'd put himself in front of me to stop. Even Ren—who might like me but didn't know me—was putting himself between us at my defense.

"She will be one of us. And he will have what he wants. Make no mistake." She said it like it was a threat, until I got a fleeting glance of an expression on her cold face.

No. Not a threat.

A warning.

Without so much as another word, she stalked out the front door. When the glass rattled with the slam, I pulled my wrist from Alistair's grip and backed up.

I wasn't mad at him, but I was wrapping my brain around everything that just happened. Alistair's mother came here at the ass end of dawn after she heard of us together. How she heard, I didn't know. Maybe from Deya herself. But either Alistair didn't speak to his mother or he didn't want her in his home, so she knew coming here would cause a scene.

She didn't have to announce the marriage. She didn't have to say anything at all. She didn't have to come here at all. If she knew about Deya's spell—which the longer I thought about it, made the most sense—then she knew we might one day come to that end. And someone wanted this? He. She said: *he will have what he wants*.

Who was this *he*, and who was he to her? Maybe *he* was Alistair's father?

In the middle of my musings, Alistair grabbed my hand—the one not holding a sword—and took it into his own. He almost cradled it, as if it were precious to him. Maybe it was.

"I didn't know she would do this. I thought I made it clear that I wouldn't go through with an arranged anything. I swear, Max."

"I know."

Alistair stood at his full height, straightening from a slight crouch that had him at eye level.

"What do you mean, 'I know?'"

I yawned before pressing the rune to shrink the blade of my athame. Within a moment, it was re-sheathed, and I was headed to what I hoped was a kitchen. "Exactly what I said. Is there coffee?"

"Yes, Majesty. There is a fresh pot in the kitchen," Ren answered, and I tried really hard not to roll my eyes at the majesty bullshit.

"Ren, we talked about this. Beignets?"

"Of course. I procured Café du Monde's first batch of the day," Ren replied, skirting around me to the oven where he pulled out a hot plate piled high with fried bliss. I was so tempted to let the majesty shit go if it got me Café du Monde beignets. I'd heard they were little bits of heaven. I couldn't wait to try one.

"Would you like to explain the 'I know' comment? I would love to know if my balls are about to be permanently removed from my body."

Alistair was being cute. After last night, there was no way I'd remove that important bit of anatomy, and he knew it. I didn't answer him until I had a steaming cup of coffee in front of me and a warm beignet on a plate. Sitting at the expansive island in the middle of the kitchen, I sipped my coffee before biting into the best thing I'd ever eaten. It was sweet but not too much, a little firmer than a donut, and so fucking good.

I may have made sex noises at a piece of fried dough, and I wasn't even a little sorry.

Alistair cleared his throat.

"Oh, sorry," I said around the beignet and sipped more coffee. "Right. I know because you told her as much and she acted like she'd heard it before. Rather recently if I was guessing, but that would just be intuition talking. She came here after hearing about us from someone, maybe even Deya herself. She probably doesn't actually want the marriage to go through, either."

Both Ren and Alistair looked confused. Men.

"She came here specifically to piss you off and do the opposite of what she asked. Duh. If she wanted us together, the best course of action was to leave us the fuck alone. By coming here, she is maneuvering us to the opposite. And the warning at the end there? Yeah. Who is she talking about? Who will have what he wants?"

Alistair sighed and poured himself a cup of coffee, sipped it, and leaned heavily on the island. "My father. Soren. He's the one who struck the deal with Abaddon."

Soren. I'd need to ask Bernadette and Andras about him. Granted, that was likely handing out a death sentence, but I wasn't too mad at that. Not if what I thought was true.

I was looking for an ancient demon with enough juice to mind-control an Alpha dragon. Who better than a wheeling and dealing criminal who was trying to force his son into an arranged marriage?

Okay, so the connection was thin at best.

"But why? What does he gain by us being..." I didn't want to say married. If I said married, then I would give a full-body shudder and maybe vomit a little.

"Married?" he answered, supplying the dreaded word.

I swallowed a sip of coffee and bit into another beignet as I nodded.

"He gets access to the royal family—what little there is left—gaining the status he feels he is *rightfully* owed," Alistair said sarcastically.

"Perfect. That means we really need to snap up Deya and get her to talk. She knows who she sold those *grigri* bags to. While we're there, we can ask her why she sold us out to your mother."

Alistair's eyebrows crawled up his forehead. "Why would she sell us out to my mother? Are you saying that my mother set us up?"

"Maybe. Maybe not. But it feels awfully coincidental, doesn't it? We're hit with that spell and somehow your mother gets wind of it? I know we weren't discreet, but we're in New Orleans. A girl making out with a guy isn't news, and it sure as shit isn't gossip worthy. Especially at this hour. Either your parents have someone watching you, or she was told by the person who did the spell."

"And why that spell?" Alistair asked. "Of all the spells she could cast, why that one?"

"We're being maneuvered, and I don't like it one bit. We need to get Deya, and I think I might have a line on how to do that."

I fished my phone out of my pocketbook, and dialed Della. When she answered, I said, "I'll give you coffee and all the beignets you can eat if you come to Alistair's house and let us explain the situation. Do not try to make me leave this city without information, Della."

I could feel her eyes narrowing through her silence. "I assume you want me to tell the boys to hang back?"

"Nope. They can come, too. I just need you to listen."

Della growled before she gave me a terse "*fine*" and hung up the phone.

"You might want to brew more coffee," I told Ren. "We've got a goddess to find."

CHAPTER SIXTEEN

"You want to do *what?*" Della asked, but I knew she heard me just fine.

I wanted to find Deya. What was so hard to understand about that?

"Your grandmother is going to set me on fire, you know that, right? Vampires are flammable, Maxima. I will burn and die because you're actively trying to get yourself killed."

I'd never known Della to be dramatic, but here we were.

"Deya Baptiste might be a goddess, but she could have killed me a hundred times over and didn't. This makes me think she might not want me dead. Now, she has information I need. Fifty-three witches are dead because of the *grigri* bags she made. Not to mention we have a dragon in human lock up, and an ancient demon using the Council as his own puppet show. I do not have the luxury of sitting on my hands because my grand-mother doesn't want dirt under my fingernails."

Protection was one thing, but I couldn't just sit there and watch people getting hurt. I'd never been able to and I sure as shit wasn't going to start now. Not with Maria trapped inside her own head. Not with so many murdered like they were nothing.

"You are going to be the death of me, I swear. And you two are no help," Della griped, chastising Aidan and Hideyo for just standing there.

"You realize she doesn't need your permission. She is Sentinel, and she has a job to do," Hideyo insisted, his tone harsher than I'd ever heard come out of his mouth. I wanted to defend Della, but the man wasn't wrong.

"And I don't see Bernadette burning you alive. She'd probably just stake you," I joked, trying to break the iron tension around her shoulders.

"Stakes," she scoffed. "How ridiculous. Anything will die if you bludgeon its heart."

That wasn't true. I wouldn't die that way, and I was pretty sure Alistair or Ren wouldn't, either. I didn't want to bring that up, though. I had a tough time figuring out why I needed a set of paladins if my bodyguards were more vulnerable than I was. Della could actually be killed. So could Aidan and probably Hideyo.

But dying wasn't the worst thing. My friend Mena had reminded me of that many times over. And now that we knew I was deathly allergic to rowan, well, maybe those bodyguards didn't seem so bad. And maybe now that Della had seen me nearly bite it—pun totally intended—she wasn't so keen on letting me out of her sight.

"I'm just going to see if I can even find the woman. If I can do that, then maybe we can talk to her. Nicely. She seems to like politeness."

"We're doomed," Aidan said under his breath, but I still heard him.

I had a giant city map spread across the island in Alistair's kitchen. An amethyst hung from a silver chain in my hand, and I was about to start scrying for a goddess. A tiny part of me thought this plan was not even a little smart, but I didn't have much else in the way of options.

What else was I going to do? Go back to Denver empty-handed? No, I didn't think so.

I drew a circle of black salt on the map. I had a feeling Deya was still in the city, but I didn't have the luxury of hunting all two hundred square miles for her. Letting the amethyst pendulum swing, I tried to locate the goddess. The black salt followed the pendulum as it swung until it fell in a general area of the Garden District, where we were.

I tried the spell again, but all I got was the vague as fuck coordinates and not much else.

Growling, I fished a phone out of my bag and dialed Barrett. If he gave me shit for calling, I was going to murder him.

"Done already?" he answered, and my gaze immediately met Alistair's as I blushed.

"I'm not talking about that with you. Maybe ever. I need you to give your phone to Atropos."

Barrett sputtered, "What?"

"Look, I need to find one of her sisters and she is the only person I can think of who can do that. Since I'm only getting vague as shit readings, I need her to narrow it down for me so I'm not searching every bit of the Garden District for a freaking goddess, mm-kay?"

"You left some things out last night, didn't you?"

I pursed my lips as I tried to think of a good way to tell him to hurry the fuck up. "I was busy. And spelled. Are you going to hand over your phone or what?"

"Why didn't you just call her yourself?"

I shrugged even though he couldn't see me, throwing my hand out in the process. "We aren't exactly best buds, Barrett. We didn't exchange numbers and I figured my pay-attention-to-this-note spell would be rude."

"Fine. Here she is."

Atropos' voice sounded down the line, bitchy as ever. "Maxima. Why are you calling me?"

"I need to find your sister. Do you know where she is?" Direct. To the point.

"I have a lot of siblings, Maxima. You're going to have to narrow it down." No shit, she had a lot of siblings. She had—or used to have—thousands of them.

"Deya Baptiste. Keres. Goddess of violent deaths. Currently residing in the murder capital of the United States. That sister."

Silence reigned for about half a minute, and I figured Atropos was either thinking through her mental Rolodex of siblings or stunned stupid.

"She's in Lafayette Number One. Where she always is because she was banished there ages ago."

I remembered getting knocked out by magic dust nowhere near Lafayette Number One. And the cemetery she had me in? That was in the French Quarter. Yeah... Atropos needed to check Deya's tether.

"Umm... she slipped her leash, then. Because if you think she can't leave, you are wrong. She knocked me on my ass in the middle of an alley, and I was nowhere near that cemetery."

"You don't say?" Atropos growled, and I was kinda glad I wasn't Deya at that moment.

"I do say. Where is she? Deya has information I need, like the name of the demon responsible for all this bullshit. She made those *grigri* bags, she damn near killed me. And someone paid her to do it."

More silence as Atropos digested the information. I was under the impression that anything having to do with death, Atropos would be in the know, but maybe that wasn't the case.

"She is currently in the cemetery, and I'll do you one better. I'll make sure she can't leave whatever tomb she's using as a home base. It'll be up to you to find her, though."

That was something at least.

"Thank you."

"A word to the wise: Deya is not allowed to take lives, so if you know what is good for you, don't take hers, either. Do you understand?" Atropos' cold voice sent shivers down my spine.

I got her warning loud and clear.

"I hadn't planned on trying to kill a goddess, but thanks for the warning."

"What you plan and what actually happens are hardly ever similar, Maxima."

She wasn't wrong.

"I'll do what I can," I conceded, knowing that was the best I could hope for.

"I suppose that will just have to do."

A faint bit of shuffling came over the line and Barrett's voice smacked me upside the head. "Goddess of violent deaths. Are you out of your bloody mind?"

I took a second to think about it.

"Maxima!"

"No?"

"Your grandmother is going to set me on fucking fire, you know that, right?" Barrett griped.

"Funny, Della said the same thing." Was that me snickering? Maybe. But the two of them were being the biggest pair of overdramatic ninnies ever.

"It's not funny."

"It's a little funny. Deya had roughly a thousand chances to kill me and she didn't. She had me in a warded circle tied to a chair. She could have killed me a hundred times over. You know what she did instead? Hit me and Alistair with a love spell. While I'm not going to just walk in there without backup, I'm not as concerned as you are."

I was a little concerned. Hell, I wasn't stupid. Deya not only made the *grigri* bags that damn near killed me, she also took me out with a puff of fucking dust, so there was that.

"Now I have a goddess to question, so do you have any other grievances you wish to air, or can I go?"

All I got back was a grumble.

"I love you, too. Say hi to Marcus for me."

Barrett gave me a reluctant goodbye and hung up. The man was twelve hundred years old and I was probably giving him his first gray hair.

"I've got a location. Who wants to do a little grave robbing?"

I WAS NOT A FAN OF CEMETERIES. IT DIDN'T matter how many times I'd been near one, I shuddered every single time. I didn't like cities like New Orleans or Savannah, not just because they were witch havens, but because they had too many dead just sitting there piling up on top of each other. The ley lines beneath New Orleans were hotter than a nuclear reactor.

Lafayette Number One was a tourist attraction, crowded with people looking to see the places where books were set, or movies were filmed.

Humans.

Della had to persuade the local police to insist that there was a gas leak and clear out the entire place. Not that there was even natural gas in this section of the city or that there would ever be gas lines underneath a cemetery. Whatever comforting lie the humans needed to hear to get the fuck out, I was totally fine with.

Now we just needed to find the goddess. Easy-peasy.

The biggest problem with this particular cemetery—or any others in this town—was nothing was organized. It was like a corn maze of death. Yes, there were rows, but they ended abruptly only to fork off into a dozen different directions.

And there was no hope of GPS helping me out. A human might think their signal was crapping out on them. I knew better. There was too much energy from the corpses of hundreds if not thousands of dead to interfere with anything with a battery.

Aces.

"You don't have to do this, you know. We could try to figure it out another way," Della offered as I looked up from my paper map and eyed the entrance to the cemetery like a coiled snake.

"Not fast enough. Look, don't discourage me right now. Just stick with Aidan and Ren, okay? Hideyo will be with Alistair and me. We'll come in at the Sixth Street entrance and meet in the middle. Not that this map is even a little bit to scale, but whatever."

Della grumbled something about being burned alive as she moved into position with Aidan and Ren, but I just didn't have the patience to convince her otherwise. The dead made me uncomfortable in my skin.

It wasn't bloodlust, but it was something like it. There was a power calling to me, begging me to hold it, play with it, and I just knew that if I let myself, it would turn bad. That didn't mean I didn't want to follow the feeling. Something told me that the incessant call for violence and blood was Deya—her power gearing up something awful.

It was the middle of the day in New Orleans, but as

soon as we crossed the boundary into the cemetery, the day turned to night. It couldn't have been later than ten in the morning, but the moon was above us now. When I finally got smart enough to turn back, the entrance to the street was gone, a tomb stood in place of where it once was.

"That isn't creepy at all," Alistair muttered.

"Can you feel that?" I asked, wondering if the call for violence was just me.

"Feel what?" Hideyo piped up, gripping the hilt of his sheathed sword tight enough to make the leather creak.

I had a hard time putting the feeling into words. "It's like a call for violence, and it's coming from there," I said, pointing to what I hoped was the east, but with the artificial night and moon, I couldn't be a hundred percent certain.

Alistair's warm hand in the middle of my back eased some of my fear, but I still wasn't quite comfortable with the wrath calling for me. "Follow it, love. We'll watch your back."

Pulling an athame from its sheath, I pressed the hidden rune to expand the blade. I didn't feel comfortable walking through this place without it, but I left a hand free just in case I needed to cast. I was ten feet into the first row when I felt the violence rise in me. A hooded figure appeared at the corner of a large crypt and then disappeared. I didn't know if he was hidden or had traveled?

I should have been able to see through glamours, but the ones Deya made for her acolytes were expert-level sorcery. Narrowing my eyes, I squinted into the night, looking for a shimmer in the air that would give one of them away.

Unable to see anything, a fire in me peaked.

"Fuck this," I muttered. "Back up guys and stay behind me."

"What—" Hideyo began, but Alistair grabbed him by the leathers and moved the kitsune just in time for me to snap my fingers.

Gathering the ambient magic in the air, I snapped my right hand while whispering a little Latin.

"*Somnum*," I murmured, hearing the thuds of Deya's acolytes as they hit the pavement.

"That's one way to do it," Alistair muttered.

I shrugged. "Sorry, I should have given you both more warning, but their glamours were too strong. I guess that's what you get when you have a goddess running the show. I think the way is clear, but keep your eyes peeled."

I also hoped I hadn't put Della, Aidan, and Ren to sleep, but I doubted the spell was strong enough to cover the whole block.

Moving forward, I stepped over hooded figures, following the pull that yanked on my baser instincts.

I heard the clash of blades before I saw the form of a man attacking Hideyo. His swords were a blur of steel, as he fought the hooded man. And something about that yanked harder at the wrath in me. I wanted the attacker to die. I wanted to snap his neck, and when Hideyo cut him down, I was actually disappointed I didn't get a chance to hurt him. And a tiny part of me wanted to hurt Hideyo for taking away my quarry.

"Maxima, love," Alistair murmured, pulling my chin to face him. I met his beautiful blue gaze and flinched at the concern.

I was not okay. Not even a little. If this was how Deya's power worked, I wanted no part of it.

"We have to move faster. Her power is calling and it's messing with my mind."

"Ready to run, then?" Alistair asked, snagging my hand and pulling me along.

The crypts were a maze of monoliths, but soon, I overtook Alistair and ran full speed toward that awful bit of wrath that yanked at my insides. That was until it threatened to overwhelm me.

All I wanted was blood on my sword. I wanted broken necks and bloody hands. I wanted shattered bones and ripped flesh. Was this what a Keres really was? Was this what she was capable of?

"Can you feel it?" I asked again, but Hideyo and Alistair shook their heads. "You have to stay back. I don't know what I'll do."

Hideyo shot that down as soon as it came out of my mouth. "No, Max, we'll follow but farther back. Maybe it'll give us time to run if you turn murdery."

It was the best I could ask for under the circumstances.

"Try to keep me from killing her?"

Alistair and Hideyo shared a dubious look. Yeah, I didn't see that going too well, either. Rather than debate it, I turned and kicked in the crypt door. A smiling Deya was on the other side, sitting on her scarlet high-backed chair. The same one she had at the other cemetery.

"You rang?" I said snidely. And I had planned to be respectful. Shit.

"I'd say you rang first. Binding me to this crypt? Rude."

Smiling, I shrugged.

"I didn't do that. Atropos says hi, though. What, no chair for me? That's okay," I said as I snapped my fingers, pulling an ottoman from nowhere and taking a load off. "Where were we? Oh, that's right. The demon's name. I would like it, please."

Deya's smile turned rueful. "Doing my sister's bidding. How do her boots taste, I wonder?"

"Says the woman confined to a crypt. By the way, is

this wrath feeling you? If so, bravo. No wonder this city is practically killing each other. You're doing a fabulous job, sweetie."

Deya huffed, crossing her legs and throwing them over one of the armrests. "What will really bake your noodle is, am I here because it's the most violent city, or is it so violent because I'm here?" She shrugged. "A question for the ages."

If I had to guess, it was door number two. I had no illusions Deya was responsible for more than a little death. It was her calling after all.

"Your stalling tactics are epic, darling, but I still want that name."

"You don't want it. You *need* it. These are two very different things. You want tamales and bourbon and world peace, but you *need* violence. It's what makes you. Everywhere you go there are storms and blood, and honestly, I'm inclined to give you what you need. If you do me a favor, that is."

Another favor? Other than not killing her? Doubtful.

"I want Atropos to lift the leash. I want to go anywhere in the city. Not just this cemetery and not this crypt."

And how much of her influence would taint the rest of the world if she got what she wanted? Would more people feel this wrath, this call to kill?

"Not if humans feel like this when you're around."

She huffed again and rolled her eyes, the wrath fled me in an instant. "They don't. I don't do that anymore. That was just a little incentive for you to come here. I didn't infect your friends, now did I?"

"Anymore" was the sticking point, and she knew it. She was banished for a reason—not that I knew what it was, but still.

"I can ask, but you know your sister. She'll do what she wants to."

Deya twirled a braid around her finger, giving me a long-suffering sigh. "If that's the best you can do, I guess."

Stalling. Why was this woman always stalling? "The name, Deya."

"Fine, but you aren't going to like it."

I'd be the judge of that.

"Soren Quinn."

She was right. I didn't like it at all.

CHAPTER SEVENTEEN

Of course the man I was looking for was Alistair's dad. I mean, why not?

"I suppose he thought I would be a good ally. With a past like mine, anything involving the violent death of innocents would be a no-brainer. My sisters and I used to be a vindictive, bloodthirsty lot. We took lives that weren't ours to take. Soren asked me to make up the bags, and I did it. He said he could get me free from my banishment. And he did for about two days. Now I'm stuck again, and the only way out is to help you."

Help me? Deya Baptiste didn't want to help me. She only wanted to help herself.

But if she was coughing up information, I wasn't going to dissuade her.

"From what I can gather, Soren wants to dismantle

the Council. I don't know why exactly, but I do know he wants to use his son to do it. Something about ruling Hell. That was all I could glean from him in the short time we were together."

Maybe she was a mind reader like Clotho, or perhaps she could see past what was to be.

"Why should I trust anything you say? You're the queen of distraction, and I wouldn't put it past you to send me on a wild goose chase."

Her lips twisted, a rueful smile mixed with chagrin. "Because it benefits me to tell you the truth. If I lie, you won't talk to Atropos for me. And... I might be feeling a little bit of guilt. Had I known the magic would have affected the shifters like that I—"

I cut her off. "You would have done the same damn thing, don't lie to me."

"Make no mistake, I would have still made the bags. I just would have added protection for the shifters. Those people didn't deserve what was done to them."

"Are you sure it was Soren? If I go back to the Council with this information, it's going to cause more than a few waves. I want you to be sure."

How was I going to tell Alistair that it was his father that caused those deaths? How the fuck was I going to explain that?

"Yes, Deya. Do be sure," a crisp British voice called out. *Shit.*

The scrape of stone on stone should have heralded Alistair's entrance to the crypt, but there was nothing. He moved quieter than I had anticipated.

"You knew your father was bad news, Alistair. I assumed you suspected him already."

"You and I both know it is one thing to suspect someone, and quite another to learn he was directly responsible for fifty-three deaths right under my bloody nose," he gritted out.

The edges of Alistair's flesh took on the cast of blackened charcoal, proof positive that his rage was getting the best of him. Not that I could blame him. Had my father turned out to be a flaming asshole, I'd be in the same boat. Oh, wait. I was in the same boat.

"Let's just take this information back to the Council. If they didn't hold Andras' sins against me, I highly doubt they'd hold Soren's against you."

Alistair's laugh was mirthless.

"Have you any idea what it has been like to have that man as my father? He's practically the reason Ethereals as a whole think demons are worthless miscreants. And no matter what I've done, he still manages to find a means to worm his way into it and turn it to complete shite."

Deya's laugh was just as joyless as Alistair's.

"Do you want to tell him, or shall I?" she asked me, and I winced. If Alistair was about to phase with just his father being named, he'd probably lose his mind once he found out his father wanted to use his son as a stepping-stone to dismantle the Council.

"Tell me what?"

Deya, unable to hold in the tea any longer, spilled. "He wants to dismantle the Council and use you to do it. He also wants to unseat her family and rule Hell."

A wave of heat whooshed through the room as Alistair's phase went from minimal to full-blown in an instant. Horns pushed up from his shoulders, punching through his jacket as if it was a personal affront. His skin blackened like soot—glowing runes carved into his skin like liquid fire. His eyes burned like hot embers, the fire in them full of wrath.

Yep, Alistair had lost the last bit of his mind, and if I didn't act soon, he was going to try and murder a goddess. Without much thought on my part—because I was hella flammable and Alistair was practically made of fire—I thrust myself between his advancing form and Deya.

"You need to calm your shit, Knight. She's giving us the information we need, and Atropos wants her alive."

His eyes blazed brighter as he spoke through gritted teeth. "I don't give a fuck what Atropos wants. Move, Max."

"No. I didn't just get you for you to sign your own

death warrant now. Sorry, you're just going to have to take your rage out on your dad. I'll help."

Alistair's growl was something out of nightmares, but I didn't show even a little bit of fear. "Do I need to put you in another circle? Because I'll do it and damn the consequences."

He stopped moving forward, but it didn't look like he was happy about it.

Then I couldn't see him at all because I had a wraith in front of me for about a second before Aidan's hands closed over my arms, and I was pulled from the crypt.

Via traveling.

I *hated* traveling.

When we landed outside of the crypt, I stumbled to the pavement and lost my beignets.

"Prick," I gasped before puking again in a potted plant in a stone urn. Traveling felt like I was being ripped into tiny little pieces and put back together wrong.

Aidan waved a phone in front of my face, his expression a mask of stony silence.

"Hello? Aidan? Did you hear me?" Teresa's voice sounded through the receiver.

"Mom?"

"Max, honey. You need to get back here right now. Maria is awake."

Maria is awake. I'd been dreaming of hearing that for

the last twenty-four hours. Had it only been a day? I was already a mass of goo on the pavement, but those three words made me wilt even farther with relief.

"I'm coming, okay? You tell her I'm coming."

Teresa's relieved laugh trilled through the line, and for the first time in maybe ever, I wanted to hug my mother. "I will."

I hung up and handed the phone back to Aidan.

"A simple 'Maria's awake' would have done the job. I hate traveling."

Managing to peel myself off the ground, I watched with amazement as the night turned back into day. Deya had lifted whatever spell she had on the place, at least. Unless Alistair killed her...

I pushed my way through Della and the boys to make sure he hadn't done just that. What I found was a still-phased Alistair eyeing Deya like she was a snake and Deya paying him exactly zero attention.

"My sister is awake, let's go," I called to him and watched in amazement as his body reverted to his normal form. Heat still shimmered off of him, but I'd take it.

Alistair turned to me, confusion on his face. Okay, so maybe I might have forgotten to mention Maria's condition in the middle of all this. Whoops?

"She's been asleep this whole time? It's been a week."

"Yes. And now she's awake. Let's. Go." I turned to Deya. "I'll talk to Atropos. I can't promise anything, but I will do what I said I would."

Deya nodded. "I believe you. It's in your nature to be honest."

Whatever that meant.

A sort of sadness fell over her face for a split second. "Good luck with your sister, Max."

I wanted to say the sentiment was comforting, but it wasn't at all.

IN THE END, WE USED A DOORWAY TO GET BACK home. There were too many of us who couldn't travel instantaneously, and no one but Della could handle Aidan's form of transportation. My casting room was lit up with candles. My grimoires were strewn all over the place like Ian and Teresa had been hard at work, trying to figure out Maria's condition. As soon as I stepped from my casting room, I knew something wasn't quite right.

The house was silent.

No ruckus in the kitchen for the woman who hadn't eaten in a week, no shower upstairs. No talking at all.

I pulled out my athame, extending the blade as I took the stairs two at a time. Now that we knew Soren was on the loose and likely had an unhealthy obsession with both his son and me, I was expecting the worst.

What I got was an empty kitchen and a silent living room.

That's not to say that the living room was empty. No, Ian sat on the couch, quietly sipping bourbon in the dark. I didn't know why it physically hurt everything in me to see that.

Maria was awake. So why did his face look like a car crash?

"Ian."

Was that my voice? Was that all the pain I'd been carrying around with me spilling from my lips with that one word?

Ian sipped his bourbon, set it on a side table, and then brought both his fists down on my coffee table, snapping it to bits.

It wasn't the shock of Ian tearing up my living room that shook me to my core. It was every possibility of why he could be losing his fucking mind. The athame slipped from my fingers, and I felt Alistair holding me up as my knees threatened to drop me. Aidan went to his brother, trying to get him to calm down, but it took Aidan, Ren, and Hideyo to make him stop ripping the place apart.

Blinking furiously, I forced tears back and stood on my own. Step by step, I walked to Maria's room, ready to find her dead. Ready to see the absolute worst.

It made me regret every second I spent away from her. It made me regret all the years I watched her from afar, unable to make contact because of who I was.

When I reached the threshold, I was more than a little surprised to see Teresa's dry eyes and Maria sitting up in bed.

Then everything became clear.

Since the ordeal with Micah, I'd been able to see more than glimpses of energies. As a child, I'd get flashes of it, but as I aged, I often knew what people were before they said. Since Micah, those flashes turned into something more.

Every species of Ethereal had a different energy.

The motes of magic around Maria weren't even in the realm of witch.

No.

The swirl of black and orange was more telling than the look on my mother's face.

Whatever Bernadette had done to save Maria hadn't worked.

All that we had done to stop Elias hadn't worked. Everything we'd sacrificed, every life we'd taken.

None of it did a damn bit of good.

Because there was a demon inside my sister's body, and I couldn't think of a damn thing to fix it.

CHAPTER EIGHTEEN

The demon inside my sister's body refused to look at me. I couldn't tell if that was because she was a demon in a circle—demons tended to hate that—or if she was confused about how she'd gotten here.

I doubted the second option. Elias made a deal with a demon—maybe more than one. She had to know where she was. She had to know what she'd stolen from us. She had to know what she'd done.

To me.

To my family.

To Ian.

To everyone who had ever loved her, ever known her.

A line of black salt surrounded the bed, sigils drawn with chalk marked the boundary, kind of like a double circle. Mom wasn't taking any chances then.

"Did you put up the circle before or after she woke up?"

The sheer fact that I could say those words proved I had control. Because I wanted to rip the room apart like Ian had. I wanted to rip that soul out of my sister and watch as it writhed in my hands. Luckily, I had better control than that.

Teresa looked away from Maria's face—the first time she'd done so since I walked in—and seemed to think about it for a second.

"When she started to rouse. After everything that happened and how long it took her to wake…" She trailed off, shaking her head. Teresa was going to break and soon.

She needed something to do.

"I want you to do me a favor, okay? Call Barrett and Bernadette. They might be able to help."

Did I actually believe that? Not in the least.

Was I going to tell my mother that? Absolutely not.

"You're right. They might have seen this before," she murmured, proof positive denial was a powerful thing.

Teresa stood and passed me at the doorway. I wanted to hug her, the grief in her so potent, I could see it weighing her down. But I knew better. If I hugged her, she'd break just like I would, and the rage was all I had to keep me going.

I skirted the circle, taking Teresa's seat. I couldn't

look at the bed yet, couldn't meet eyes that were Maria's but not.

"When she was born, I was so excited," I began, my voice nearly a whisper. "I didn't get to play with other children much, and when Teresa told me that I was going to be a big sister, I couldn't wait. Teresa—my mother—didn't like me or didn't understand me or she was afraid of me. And sometimes looking at me, she'd get this expression on her face like it hurt her to look at me. So, when Maria was born, all I wanted was someone, anyone, to look at me like I was something." I swallowed hard, the lump in my throat growing by the second.

"From the day she was born, she was my best friend. She was mischief and wonder and giggles. She was the only person to love me. She was my only friend. My only family." I glanced up then, taking in all of Maria's features that weren't hers anymore. The press of her lips, the set of her shoulders, the wild, frightened eyes.

The tears I tried to hold in crested my lids, flowing down my cheeks.

"So when you sit there in her skin, wearing her face, I want you to understand what you took. You took the first person to love me. The first person to show me what family was. The first friend I ever had in the world, my purpose when I had nothing else to live for."

I couldn't go on, telling this demon what Maria

meant to me. I'd only had her in my life for such a short time. Only a handful of years, really. And the rest had been me on the outside looking in on a sister who couldn't ever really know me because of what I was.

"So you'd better pray to whatever deity you find holy that I can get her back. Because I didn't abandon my sister when I had nothing and no one, and I sure as shit won't be doing it now."

The demon started laughing then. But it wasn't a happy laugh. No, it was a half-hysterical almost cry that chilled me to the bone.

Tears welled up in the demon's eyes—Maria's eyes— as her whole body shook, her hands practically vibrating. She curled her fingers under, balling them into fists, but she didn't stop that awful keening. When those horrid sounds stopped, she began to cry, but as she did it, she began to speak.

"I didn't ask for this. I don't want this. *I didn't ask for this,*" she screamed, her hands rough on her own face as if she'd like to scratch her skin off but didn't want to hurt the body.

"I hope that's true, because if I have my way, you'll go back to where you came from."

Then I got up and waited in the kitchen for Barrett and Bernadette, and I prayed to no one in particular that my sister could be saved.

· · ·

I WAS PUTTING MY CASTING ROOM TO RIGHTS when Bernadette and Barrett arrived. My apothecary cabinet was a complete mess, and once the grimoires were in order, I needed to fix that. Then I needed to dry more herbs, and maybe I needed to charge more of my crystals or something. Maria was always on me about that. I never had enough charged crystals or dried herbs. I didn't have cleansed tarot decks or a proper altar, either.

And I was focusing on making sure everything was organized and put back together rather than what Bernadette and Barrett might tell me. Teresa was more versed in the possession angle than I was, and she wasn't too optimistic. What news could they give me that wasn't as clear and concise as Teresa's face when she told me she called them to help us?

Alistair and Della had tried to talk to me, but I couldn't seem to articulate what I was feeling, and if I caught even a glimpse of pity, I was going to lose it.

But it wasn't Barrett or Bernadette who came to get me.

"How you doing, kid?" Marcus called from the open door. Not a stitch of pity was on his face, but I knew it was a mask. What else could it be?

"Shitty. You?"

Barrett and Marcus had gotten to know Maria in the

six precious months I had with her. I knew they were feeling this, too.

"I'm doing just a little bit better than you are. They're ready if you want to be there. No one will blame you if you don't. The way Barrett talks about it, this isn't going to be pretty."

I knew they were planning an exorcism. It was just about the only thing they could do. But from what I'd read in my strewn grimoires, it was nothing like the movies. It wasn't a bit of Latin, a priest, and some holy water.

If only it were that easy.

From the description in my books, an exorcism loosened the binding of a soul with a body, and more often than not, the host ended up dead. I knew what was at stake, but I didn't know if I could handle the consequences should it pan out that way.

My brain was pitifully trying to come up with alternatives to what was coming. Or maybe search for something the surviving exorcism witches had that the others didn't.

So far, there wasn't anything of note.

"I want to be there. I'm just—"

Marcus leaned on the doorframe and finished my sentence. "Trying to gather the courage?"

How did he always know?

"Maybe," I said from my disarrayed altar, watching as Alistair joined Marcus in the doorway.

Alistair gave me a sly smile and held out a cut crystal glass filled with amber liquid. "If I give you a glass of bourbon and a hug, you think you can pull your shit together?"

I waggled my hand at him.

"Good enough. Come on, love. We have a job that needs doing. Drink your courage, and let's go."

Reluctantly, I stood, dragging my feet as I reached for the bourbon. Alistair passed the glass over and wrapped an arm around me.

"We're not giving up on her, love. Don't you, either," he murmured against my hair before dropping a kiss to my temple.

I wanted to be optimistic, but I couldn't quiet the voice in the back of my head that said I should have stayed home.

I let Alistair pull me upstairs to Maria's room. The bed had been moved to the centermost point in the room, a circle of salt, herbs, and small bones surrounded the bed. A square of the same ingredients surrounded the circle, white pillar candles sitting at the four corners. The demon wearing Maria was at the center with Ian, a stethoscope around his neck. His face still looked like a car crash, but he had a little hope left in him, which was something I was lacking. Aidan, Della, and Hideyo were at the corners of the room, weapons drawn and ready.

Barrett and Bernadette were finishing up their preparations. When Bernadette saw me, she wrapped me up in a bone-crushing hug.

"I'm so sorry, Max. I thought I helped. I thought—"

"I know. We did what we could. That's all anyone can ask of us, right?" I didn't blame Bernadette or Teresa or Andras or anyone else.

I just wanted this mess to not be true. I just wanted it to be fixed.

"We're ready to start," Barrett murmured, elbowing his way into our little huddle so he could hug me. "We've been talking to the demon. She is more than willing to release the body. Apparently, Elias summoned her without consent and never made a deal with her. All she wants is to go back home."

That was in line with what she said earlier that I may or may not have been too cognizant to hear.

"Ian is monitoring Maria's vitals. He'll be here to make sure her body can handle it. Too many exorcisms haven't had medical staff on hand. This will make sure we don't go too far," Barrett added, trying to ease my worry. "Alistair is here to make sure the vacating soul goes back where it belongs—the rest of your paladins are here as backup. You and Teresa will act as a familial bond, calling to Maria's soul to expel the demon's. Have you studied the exorcism spells?"

I nodded. "What point do you want me at?"

I had to ask because it wasn't like I was an air or water witch. I didn't draw on anything but myself. My position in the circle was up to the witch casting it.

"I think north will do given your penchant for earth-quakes. Teresa will be south, Barrett east, and I'll take west. Ian will be in the center with Maria's body."

North signified earth. I could work with that. Not that this was like any witch circle I'd ever been a member of—not that I'd been part of many witch circles in my day. Not too many circles consisted of two-and-a-half witches and a demon and a half.

We took our positions, and Barrett began the incantation.

"*Projiciam vos a facie mea. Hoc corpore dimittere. Vade exiit daemonium relinquunt corpus. Vade exiit ad inferos.*"

The translation to English was rough, the form of Latin more obscure than I was used to, but the gist of it was, "Get your ass back to Hell and leave this body alone."

I could respect that level of directness in an exorcism.

Repeating Barrett's words, I added my magic to the working.

"Projiciam vos a facie mea. Hoc corpore dimittere. Vade exiit daemonium relinquunt corpus. Vade exiit ad inferos."

The candles flared, their flames ratcheting higher as Bernadette joined in.

"Projiciam vos a facie mea. Hoc corpore dimittere. Vade exiit daemonium relinquunt corpus. Vade exiit ad inferos."

When Teresa's voice joined the cadence, the flames reached waist-high.

"Projiciam vos a facie mea. Hoc corpore dimittere. Vade exiit daemonium relinquunt corpus. Vade exiit ad inferos."

Salt and herbs and tiny bones swirled at the perimeter of the circle.

The demon flinched, and then her whole body flailed. It looked like someone was yanking her soul from her chest—which I guessed was exactly what we were doing. I felt a tiny bit of hope at that moment. Each revolution of the spell ramped up the flames, and it wasn't until she started screaming, that my hope died.

If the demon wasn't fighting this, why was it hurting her?

Maria's body shook violently, and then she retched, blood spilling from her mouth. Instantly, I quit my incantation, praying the others would follow suit.

"Stop, stop, *stop*," I screamed as the room quieted, and the flames died.

Aidan tossed Ian his medical bag, and he started working on Maria's body.

But I knew. I knew it before Bernadette said it. "This shouldn't happen. Hearts stopping, maybe, but... This is wrong. It's like Maria isn't there at all."

Because she wasn't.

And I knew exactly where her soul was.

In Hell. Where she'd been all along.

CHAPTER NINETEEN

"Darkness and screaming. I'd thought she was in a dream state not that—" I couldn't finish that sentence.

I hauled ass out of Maria's room back down the stairs to my casting room. All this time I'd been trying to find the demon responsible. Well, I'd summoned his son to a circle by accident. I wondered what I could do on fucking purpose.

I had a vial of salt in my hand, and I was two-point-five seconds away from drawing a circle on my casting room floor and summoning his ass when Marcus, Alistair, and Barrett caught up with me.

"Don't you fucking dare, Maxima," Barrett ordered as I flicked the cork stopper off the salt vial.

I felt my eye twitch, and outside there was a crack of thunder so fierce, it shook the house.

"He stole my sister's soul. He has her in Hell and has been doing Fates know what for a week, Barrett. He's responsible for the deaths of fifty-three witches, the brainwashing of a Council member, and Fates know what else. If I can get him contained, I'd be doing this realm and every other realm a favor."

"Only to be executed right alongside him." That was from Alistair, and he said it like the words burned as they came up.

"Why? Because I was born an Arcadios witch?" The betrayal in that statement stung. Why were they just standing there? Maria was in Hell right this second.

She was screaming.

Barrett sighed, pinching his brow in his fingers and shook his head. It was Marcus who answered for him.

"It was outlawed for a reason. It's one thing to do it by accident. It's a whole other animal to do it on purpose. And you want us to look the other way? Baby girl, we can't do that."

His soft, gentle steps across the room hit me like knives, and when he took the salt vial from my loose fingers, I wanted to scream.

"She's *screaming*, Marcus. My baby sister is screaming in Hell. If I can't summon him, I have to do something else."

Didn't he know? I'd never left my sister behind. Not

when I was a child with nothing and no one. Not when Elias had her, and none of the times in between.

"No one is saying give up. Just don't sign a death warrant right this second. We—"

I cut Marcus off. "You're just telling me to leave the man who did this to her alone."

"What did you say to me when I was going to go after Deya, Max?" Alistair murmured, his arm wrapping around my chest from behind. "'I didn't just get you for you to sign your own death warrant now.' Don't do this, love. We'll figure out another way."

Wet hit my eyes as I let my head fall back to his shoulder. If I couldn't summon Soren, I would have to figure out another way.

All I knew was none of these men were going to like what I was going to come up with.

THERE WAS NO OTHER WAY AROUND THE WAIT for the demon to wake up. After Ian stabilized Maria's body, the whole of us waited for her parasite to recover enough for consciousness.

That was an uncharitable thought, and I wasn't proud of it. The demon didn't want to be here either, and she tried to give Maria's body back. As it stood, none of this was her fault. It didn't stop me from feeling that way, though, and it was becoming harder and harder to check myself.

Della made sure I ate, and Alistair made sure I at least attempted to sleep. Aidan and Hideyo patrolled the perimeter, and Barrett and Marcus pored over grimoires they'd retrieved from who knew where. My father had come sometime in the night to comfort Teresa, and Bernadette poured enough tea down my gullet to make me spring a leak.

The one person I thought would be here never showed up, but I never really expected him to. He had a family to look out for, and that didn't include me.

Not anymore.

A few people came that I didn't expect, however. Aurelia and Rhys showed up sometime in the middle of the night sans kiddos. A part of me wondered if this many people in my house was a punishment for wanting a full house. For lamenting at the emptiness and all the unused rooms. I didn't like being tip-toed around, and I couldn't make them stop.

All I wanted right then was for everyone to leave.

To stop hovering.

To let me plan.

But no one left me alone. Hell, if I had to guess, Aurelia was the one making sure I wasn't left alone for a single second. And as I stared into my friend's pale, pupilless eyes, I wondered how much of this she'd already seen. If she knew my sister was in Hell already. If she knew her body was dying in the next room.

I wanted to ask, but I knew better. There was a whole host of things Aurelia didn't say on any given day because she knew the outcome. A believer in free will, she didn't want to influence others.

I tried not to hold that against her. I really did.

"It's not going to turn out the way you want it to," Aurelia murmured.

I shook myself out of my plotting and refocused on her. She was sitting on the edge of my bed, holding my hand. Alistair was sitting next to me holding the other. I wondered when I'd gotten up here but decided quickly it didn't matter.

"What?"

"Your plan. The one you aren't telling anyone about? It won't turn out like you want it to. It's going to go bad."

I clenched my jaw to avoid violence. "What plan?"

"I may be a few centuries younger than you, but please don't pretend I'm stupid. You can't do what you want. It will have consequences you are not prepared to pay."

If she meant my life, I could deal with that. If it meant a lifetime—hell, a hundred lifetimes—in a null cell, I could deal with that, too.

I pulled my hand from hers and from Alistair's. I sat

up in that bed and locked eyes with my best friend. "If it was your sister, what would you do? Would you listen to a warning and give up? Or would you go ahead, knowing that it might not work out?"

Aurelia's stoic expression melted into one of pain. Her eyes welled as her mouth twisted.

Yeah, that's what I thought.

"I'd do exactly what you're going to do. Even knowing what I know."

"Then there's nothing left to say," I muttered, my voice breaking as I looked away.

Aurelia snorted. "There's more to say, just not to you." She shifted her body, staring at Alistair like he was a bug on her boot. "You will listen to her plan. You will aide her in her endeavors. You will hate every single facet of this plan. But I expect you to bring her out of this alive or die trying."

Alistair recaptured my hand, studying it for a moment before he laced his fingers with mine.

"That was always the plan."

WHEN THE DEMON INSIDE MARIA'S BODY WOKE up, she seemed devastated she was still here right along with the rest of us. The fact that she did wake up was a good sign—at least for the host body.

"It didn't work. Why didn't it work?" she asked Ian over and over again.

Each time she asked him why, it was like watching him get stabbed in the gut. Smartly, Aidan got him out of the room before he started ripping the place apart.

Bernadette took charge of the demon, and once she found out who Bernadette was, it was a free-for-all on information. Being the Queen of Hell had its perks, I guessed.

The demon—Selene—was a lower-level demon, an imp of some kind with little to no power. She was stolen from her home months ago and sold. Not that I knew what an imp even was or what they did, but trading souls for power kinda seemed like a bad thing.

Who knew there was a black market in Hell? Not this girl.

But Bernadette and Alistair knew, I could tell by their faces. The wince that came over their expressions as Selene talked about being taken and sold was all I needed to know.

"There is a demon who buys us, stealing whatever power we have. We call him *neque sanctiores animarum*. Destroyer of Souls. He uses us to power old magic. A spell with no name, no language, in a place at the edge of nothing and nowhere. It is blackness there—even for those of us who can see past the shadows." Her lip trembled as fresh tears snaked down her cheeks. She clutched the blankets tighter.

It made me wonder why she would want to go back there. Ever.

"Why would you want to go back?" Della asked, stealing the question from my brain like a mind reader.

"I don't want to go back there. I want to go home. I have a family. A life. It's nothing like this, but it's all I know."

That statement made me wonder what Hell was like for the demons. Was it just another job, another way of living? Or was it something else?

I had a feeling I was about to find out.

"Do you know the man's real name?" I probed. I had a good idea who'd taken her, but I wanted to be sure. No one was going to get on board with my plan if I didn't have evidence—confirmation from a goddess or not.

Selene nodded, but she eyed Alistair like she didn't want to say. "I saw his face when I was sold. It was the last time I saw anything until I was brought to the circle."

Alistair nodded, his jaw set. "If it's who I think it is, you can say, Selene. We'll get him. I swear it."

She twisted the covers in her hands, her jaw clenching as she seemed to gather the courage.

"Soren Quinn."

I nodded and left the room, heading back down to the casting room to get my supplies. I had his name and a location. I was a demon and a princess. I should be able to walk in there and get Maria's soul back. Shouldn't I?

And what other option did I have? Bernadette had spent all that time with Elias and didn't know who was behind all this. Too busy keeping her façade in place to dig deeper. Andras was persona non grata pretty much everywhere—including Hell.

The way Aurelia worded it, I wasn't going to be able to go with anyone but Alistair. So maybe Bernadette and Andras wouldn't want me to go. I filled vials with salt and iron shavings, others with holly water—not to be confused with holy water—and a few with the ashes of my burning tree. In a few other vials, I put my sister's hair in one—*don't ask how I got it*—and a few drops of her blood in another. I filled a velvet-lined pouch with my bounty and headed back upstairs.

Rifling through my weapons stash, I picked my favorite bladed implements and got dressed, tossing my hair into a tight braid.

When I made it back downstairs, my friends were waiting for me, but it was my mother who stopped me on the last step.

"You had better not be doing what I think you're doing, Maxima."

I snorted out a laugh before pushing past her. "What do you think I'm doing?

"Going into Hell, child," Bernadette answered my question. "That realm is not for you."

"Either I'm a demon or I'm not. Either I'm Princess or I'm not. Either I'm Sentinel or I'm not," I fired back, tired of all of the double-talk and riddles. "Either you're going to tell me why or I'm going. You pick. Give me a good reason why I can't go."

"You don't know the way," she whispered, skirting around me to bar my way to the door.

"I have a guide."

Bernadette looked over my shoulder where I knew my parents were standing. "I haven't had the time to tell you all my secrets, Maxima. There are things you don't know and…"

"Are any of those things more important than getting Maria's soul back? Don't answer that, because I'll tell you now that they aren't."

"Very well," Bernadette murmured, resigning herself to my half-cocked plan. "Who is going to lead you?"

Alistair joined me in facing my grandmother down, lacing his fingers with mine. "I will, my Queen."

Bernadette nodded, moving out of our way.

That was way too easy.

"Oh, Knight?" Bernadette called to our backs before we could make a break for it.

There it was.

"If you get a chance? Murder that son of a bitch father of yours, will you? Consider it a freebie."

Oh, she didn't need to worry about that. If I had my way, there wouldn't be anything left of Soren Quinn.

Not even ashes.

CHAPTER TWENTY

It was one thing to say you were going to Hell, it was quite another to actually go there. There were several entrances to that particular realm, but only a few we could actually go through without dying first. Being demons, we didn't need the more drastic methods of entry, a door in Aether would do just fine.

Funnily enough, I'd once told Caim that I would never go looking for the door I was currently searching for. It figured it would be Maria to make a liar out of me. I supposed since I wasn't looking for the door exactly, it didn't fall into the realm of lying. I was being led—there was a difference.

"Are you absolutely certain you want to do this?" Alistair asked, the first time he'd voiced any concern whatsoever about this bullshit plan.

I had to give him credit where it was due, he listened to Aurelia's every word.

"No, this is a terrible plan that will probably end in my ruin, but I'm gonna do it to get my sister back. Sound good?"

Alistair stopped at a door I'd never noticed in a hallway I'd never traversed. There were a lot of corridors in Aether, more hidden than not. The door itself was unremarkable. No carvings etched into the frame, not an inch of prettiness or ornament. If that was the door to Hell, I worried some poor soul would end up where they didn't belong.

"No, it sounds awful, and I don't like it one bit. But we're going because I refuse to be the one who tells you that you can't fight for family. Maria is your sister. If it were you instead of her, I'd be doing the same, and no one could tell me different."

Was it wrong to swoon right now? Because I really wanted to rip his clothes off and lick him in naughty places.

His smile was positively sinful as he caught my lips with his. "Later, love. When this is all over, we'll spend a week in bed, and everyone else can sod off."

Best. Plan. Ever.

"You ready?" he asked, reaching for the door handle.

Ready to go to Hell? No. Not really, but just think of all the jokes I could tell.

I was about to tell him yes when Andras appeared in front of us, blocking the door. Of course, Andras would feel the need to stop us in the most dramatic fashion possible.

"Bloody hell, man." Alistair cursed with a start, shuffling me behind him. Why he would feel the need to protect me from Andras, I wasn't sure, but knowing Andras, it really wasn't too far of a stretch.

"I want to talk to my daughter, Quinn. I know you Quinns think you have a claim to her, but you don't." Was snarling really necessary right now? Andras thought so.

"You mean the arranged marriage business? Yeah, I know all about it. Alistair and I aren't getting married, Andras. You can unclench."

Alistair drew up to his full height, which was eye to eye with my father. "I am not like my family. Do not paint me with their brush. No one will tell Max what to do. Not me, and definitely not you."

Andras seemed to consider Alistair for a moment before giving him a manly sort of nod. Was that approval? From Andras? Color me shocked.

"I still need to talk to you," Andras said to me. "Alone."

"Are you going to try to stop me? Because that won't work out so well for you. If you think Mom setting your head on fire was bad, just you wait," I threatened, cracking my knuckles.

"I'm not going to stop you."

"Fine. Alistair, can you give us a minute?"

Alistair dropped a kiss to my temple and gave us some space.

"I won't be far," he said, making sure Andras knew that he was in earshot if things got dicey.

Andras rolled his eyes in a way that seemed almost petulant.

"You aren't inured to the flames, and that is my fault. When you were an infant, your mother locked away some of your abilities. Most broke free, but..." He paused, shame coloring his face. "She locked you away—inside your own body—because I wasn't there to teach you. That's my fault. You can't go into Hell still bound. Will you turn around and move your braid?"

I wanted to be surprised, but at this point, I just wasn't. I didn't know which stories were true. Did Andras murder his father because he was killing humans? Or was it because he promised his grand-daughter away under his son's nose? Did my father care about me? Or did he abandon me to be burned at the stake?

Or did he do all of these things to protect me?

I didn't think I'd ever know for sure.

With no reason not to, I turned around, sliding my braid to the side to expose the back of my neck.

"This will hurt, my sweet girl, but it must be done."

I didn't get another warning before pain lashed through my skin like a firebomb. My scream echoed through the corridor as the ground quaked beneath our feet. The floor split, green light spilling out, until all at once, it stopped.

The pain, the earthquake, the whoosh of wind that somehow whipped through the building.

All of it.

I fell to my knees, gasping in relief.

I glanced behind me to see Andras held at the point of a scythe, with a phased Alistair looking ready to commit murder.

"It's done. It had to be done. Max, touch him while he's phased, and you'll see."

Using the wall for balance, I staggered to my feet. I wanted to believe my father. I didn't know why. He'd given me no reason to trust him. But then again, none of the people in my life had.

I reached for Alistair only to have him flinch away. "Don't, Max. You'll burn."

"Maybe, but if I do, you can hurt my dad. If not, then he did us a favor."

Alistair's lip curled. "If she gets so much as a blister, I will send you to the depths and set the hounds on you.

Then, I'll throw you in the river and let the souls feast on the scraps. I swear it, Andras."

"You know, I'm really starting to like you. You might just be worthy of my Max yet."

"I'm honored." I wanted to laugh at Alistair's deadpan delivery, but I was too busy trying to make sure I didn't burn my whole hand off.

When my hand made contact with his phased skin, I felt the warmth of it first. The fire didn't burn, but I knew it was there. Then the texture filtered in past the heat. His skin was craggy and almost brittle like charred wood, but strong, too, like stone or some sort of mineral. It was like he was made of embers.

I ran my fingers over the smoldering sigils carved into the flesh of his cheek and then pulled it back to check for blistering. Nothing.

"I ought to punch you in the face for letting me get burned at the stake. That shit hurt."

Andras pinched the edge of Alistair's scythe, pushing it away from his neck, taking a healthy-sized sidestep away from the blade.

"Yeah, well, you would have met Soren much earlier if I hadn't. Be glad, child. At least now you have a fighting chance. I'd go with you, but if I go, I can't come back. It's the price I had to pay for killing Abaddon."

It was now or never. If I was going to find out why he did what he did, I had to ask now.

"Did you kill him because he was hurting people, or was it because of me?"

Andras' smile was sad. "Both, kid. A healthy dose of both."

I supposed that vague as fuck answer would have to do.

"Here," he said, holding out a hand. I opened mine underneath it, and he dropped a handful of gold coins into it. "For the ferry."

Without so much as a word, he snatched me into a hug, kissing my hair as he did so, and then he was gone.

I opened my hand to inspect the six heavy coins. Around the edge, there were sigils I didn't know. At the center was an upside-down triangle over an inverted star with another six-pronged sigil underneath.

"That's Lilith's seal," Alistair said. "It should buy you passage both ways."

I hadn't thought of passage at all. "Do you pay every time?"

Alistair shook his head, closing my fingers over the coins with his hand. "I don't require passage. I'm not allowed on the boat. Put those in your bag."

That didn't make sense to me, but I did as I was told. "Why am I going on the boat then?"

"Because you do. You don't belong in Hell, Max, and Hell will know it as soon as you step one foot into the place. You need those coins. It gives you a pass from Lilith herself. Don't lose them."

"I won't," I muttered, tightening the tie on the pouch. As an extra precaution, I whispered an anti-thieving spell on the bag and the leather tie that attached it to my belt.

Certain his warning was clear, Alistair put his hand on the doorknob and turned. The door opened to a cobblestone bridge over black water under a blood-red sky.

"Ready?" he asked.

"Lead the way."

As soon as I stepped over the threshold onto the bridge, I felt a frisson of fear race up my body. But the earth didn't quake, and fire didn't rain down from the sky. Trust me, I was seriously concerned about both happening. The door closed of its own accord and then faded from sight. Even I couldn't see where it had been.

That was not comforting.

"Where's the door? How do we get back?" Was that my lily-livered ass talking? Yes, yes, it was.

He had the nerve to chuckle at me. We were in Hell. There were zero chucklings to be had. "We have another exit planned."

"We have a plan?"

"Okay, I have a plan. You have gumption, and a 'don't give a fuck' attitude, how's that?"

I snorted. "You know, some people would say those were the same things."

Alistair grabbed my hand and started walking down the bridge. The structure was wide enough for a two-lane road. If it weren't for the complete lack of guard rails, it would almost feel safe. As it was, though, the sea underneath us seemed too close, the sky not far enough away, and the air too thick. Everything seemed too close, like in a single moment the sea could revolt and pull me under, the sky could rain down on us, the air could choke us if it wanted.

The sky itself roiled, scarlet clouds churning in the too-close shadows. The sea did the same, black waves crashed into the bridge, sending a spray up and over the stone.

I started walking faster, dragging Alistair behind me as I booked it toward land. Well, until I saw eye sockets in one of the giant cobblestones.

We were walking on skulls.

Ohshitohshitohshit.

It was then that I realized that the bridge wasn't made of stone at all, and my anxiety about being in Hell really hit me. I may or may not have speed-walked down that bridge just shy of an all-out run.

"Max." Alistair chuckled.

"You're chuckling right now? We're walking on the

dregs of people, and you're fucking laughing? What the shit, Alistair?"

"We're walking on the dregs of child murderers. I plan to relish every step of my boots, grinding their bones to dust as they're tortured somewhere in this place. As should you."

I thought about that for two-point-five seconds, and then I smiled for a second. It fell just as quickly as it came.

Tortured.

Maria's screams echoed in my head.

She was waiting for me.

CHAPTER TWENTY-ONE

I couldn't afford the luxury of walking—not when Maria was out there somewhere, wishing she could die. I may have scoffed at Alistair a bit.

When he looked confused, I explained.

"My sister is waiting for me. Likely being tortured by your father. A sense of urgency would be appreciated."

Alistair blinked at me for a second before something like chagrin passed over his face. "Got it."

If I could have run in this getup, I would have, but as it stood, I didn't want to shatter the bottles in my pouch. "Tell me again why we can't just snap our fingers and get there?"

Alistair shuddered and shook his head. "Magic doesn't work here like it does anywhere else—especially on the Earth realm. Don't use it unless you have no other choice. And your magic? You nearly tear the world apart, and that was before your father took away what-ever Teresa did to bind you."

Alistair's eyes widened as he shook his head again.

"I don't want you to snap your fingers and rip this whole place apart. No, thank you, love. I have trans-portation covered. It's not as fast as you'd like it, but it beats walking."

Alistair jutted his chin toward the end of the bridge, where a giant gate stood in the middle of a never-ending wall. On either side of the gate, the walls went on forever. The barrier itself was taller than I could quan-tify. It seemed to fade into the sky, so I hadn't noticed it as we crossed the bridge. The gate itself was made of a blackened metal threaded through with enough magic to make it light up like a flare, while the wall consisted of something different. Sooty bricks of stone—each had a sigil that I didn't know—the mortar between them shimmering faintly with magic.

"That's a big gate."

Weirdly, the gates seemed more warded than the wall itself. I wondered if Alistair could see the wall's magic dwindling. Or was it dwindling at all? Just because the magic wasn't as bright, didn't mean it wasn't as strong. Still, I didn't feel good about just letting the observation pass.

"There are hundreds of gates. This is only one of them. Luckily, I know a guy who can open it for us."

Alistair knocked three times on the enormous metal door and waited.

"You know the magic of the wall is fading, right?" I whispered the question, afraid of saying those words too loud.

Alistair's head whipped in my direction, surprise coloring his face before his expression turned knowing. "You can see it." Not a question, a statement.

I nodded, staring at my feet before glancing back to the bridge. The magic and mortar that held the bones together was fading, too. "The bridge, too, I think."

"It's been an ongoing problem. We think someone has been siphoning off the magic. We've been working on it for a while."

I gave him a mirthless laugh. "How much you want to bet your dad has a hand in this?"

There was a commotion at the door as Alistair answered me. "All my money and yours, too."

Aces.

Did I want to devote my brain power to the fact that the barrier to Hell was failing?

No, I did not.

Was I going to while I searched for my sister? Yeah, I was. "What does Bernadette say?"

"She thinks it has something to do with the barrier to Faerie. Someone might be trying to knock down the gate between them."

I had a shitload of questions.

Like, why the fuck was there a barrier between Faerie and Hell in the first fucking place? Who was responsible for that design flaw? And siphoning power? That sounded like a demon we both knew, and the more problems that came up, the more it looked like Soren was responsible for all of them.

I thought Samael was bad. Then again, he might have been in league with this asshole.

The biggest question of them all swirled like a maelstrom in my head.

What happened when the magic in the wall was gone? I had an idea, and it was not a comforting thought.

Gears turned within the gate; metal screeched as the sound of locks turning echoed through the air. The gate cracked open maybe a foot or two, and a familiar head poked out.

Felix looked a bit different since the last time I'd seen him on the dance floor of my presentation to the Fates. No longer did he have the debonair tuxedo and slicked-back hair. Now he sported fighting leathers and silver armor on the left side of his body. The silver had sigils carved in it that might designate his house or family line or maybe his commander.

"'Bout time you guys showed up. Come on, the horses are getting restless."

Horses?

Alistair led me through the gate. On the other side was a barren desert, backed by a craggy mountain range. No people, no buildings, no trees, no nothing.

Well, *no people* was a stretch. Standing next to Felix was the ever-irritated Donovan. His red hair actually resembled flames as it gave the finger to gravity and wafted above his head as if he were underwater.

Donovan held the reins to the pair of black stallions, their red eyes glowing in the perpetually dim light. The animals seemed friendly enough, and one pulled at Donovan so he could come sniff me. The horse snuffled at my ear before resting his head on my shoulder, almost like a hug. I'd never had a horse do that, so I sent a questioning glance to Donovan.

"He likes you," Donovan informed me, and was that a spark of niceness in his tone? "His name is Erebus. He will guide you to the ferry."

I reached up to the bridge of the horse's nose and ran my fingertips over the coarse black hair. "You're a handsome man, aren't you? I appreciate your help, Erebus."

Donovan looked on with approval. Huh. This was a very different reception than I'd gotten the last time we met.

"How are you these days, Donovan?"

He glanced past me, eyeing the wall like he could see the failing magics like I could.

"I've been better, but I suppose you have, too," he said and passed me the reins. "Go find your sister, Max, and good luck. And don't worry about Erebus, he'll find his way home once your task is done."

I muttered a choked "thank you" and mounted the horse. Alistair was already on his, and he waited for me to get situated before he started in on the directions.

"There will be souls that you will pass on this route. Do not converse with them. Don't even look at them. We will be going at a fast clip, so they likely won't be able to reach us. Don't stop until we get to the ferry. For any reason. This is not a safe place, Max."

I wanted to give him a "no shit" response since this was the entrance to Hell, but I didn't. He knew this realm, and I didn't. Listening and minimal lip was kind of necessary right now.

"Got it," I said softly, patting Erebus' neck.

"We're going to go fast, boy. I'll keep people off you, you worry about going as fast as you can, okay?"

Erebus tossed his head in what seemed like a nod, and we were off, the burst of speed wholly unexpected from any land animal. Honestly, it felt more like I was on a motorcycle with how fast we were going. I dared to glance behind me, and the pair of us were kicking up enough sand and dust that I couldn't even see the gate or wall anymore.

Soon we were passing people walking in the barren

nothingness toward the mountain beyond. They looked nothing like the zombies I had dreamed up in my head when Alistair went on his rant about souls trying to get us. Still, I wasn't dumb enough to think the people futilely reaching for us were up for a chat.

We were in Hell. I was here for a reason, and I'd bet they were, too. Very different ones, mind you, but still.

Reasons.

The mountain stayed in the distance as if no number of miles traversed would bring it any closer. We went on like that for what seemed like hours, and I worried the steed beneath me would tire. But Erebus kept going, churning his legs faster and faster until the faint flicker of water came into view.

The closer we got to the shore, the more he slowed. Soon, we were at a canter, approaching a crowd waiting at the tiny dock with a carved wooden boat. The water was just as black as the churning sea that slammed into the bridge, only this ocean was calm as glass.

People milled at the dock, some sitting on the ground waiting, some yelling at an impossibly tall cloaked man holding a ferryman's pole.

"I've been here forever. I want to cross!" a burly man screamed at the cloaked figure.

I assumed the cloaked man was the ferryman, and if I were dead, pissing off the man who was taking me to my final resting place wouldn't be my first way to go. Then again, if my final resting place meant torture forever, I might be acting just like the burly guy, hoping my complaining added time to my stay on this side.

Alistair halted his horse and hopped off, and I followed suit. Granted, my dismount was ungainly and not even a little graceful. Alistair took up Erebus' reins and led the horses to the shore closest to the ferryman. The horses drank from the river, and Alistair addressed the cloaked man.

"Charon, my friend," Alistair said, shoving the bellowing soul out of the way. The people behind the fallen soul murmured but didn't dare complain. "Please meet Max."

The arm of Charon's cloak reached for me, and a skeletal hand slipped out to grasp mine. There was little to no flesh left on the withered digits, but I nodded like I wasn't screaming inside my head.

"Nice to meet you, Charon."

Charon's head—or what I assumed was his head because I actually couldn't see into the cloak to make out a face—swung to Alistair.

"She is alive," he rasped, his voice like smoky gravel.

"That she is, but she has Lilith's permission to be here. She will ride the ferry with you, and I will meet you both on the other side."

"Very well. Max, do you have your payment for passage?"

I nodded and passed over two coins from my pouch, dropping them into his skeletal hand.

"Very good," he said, inspecting the coins I gave him. "Please board the ferry, and we will be off."

Alistair hugged me tight, whispering in my ear, "Remember what I said. Don't talk to anyone but Charon. Don't look at them, okay?"

"I hear you."

"Be safe, love. I'll see you on the other side."

The boat was small, closer in size to a skip than anything. There were four other passengers on my boat, two men and two women. Each of them appeared shell-shocked like they couldn't believe they were on the boat in the first place and didn't want to be there, second. I didn't blame them. I seriously doubted what was coming for them would be any better than a boat ride on calm seas. I followed Alistair's advice, not meeting the eyes of any of the passengers, and smartly, I sat in the back closest to Charon as we shoved off from the shore.

Everyone seemed to give the ferryman a wide berth, but not me. I was burning with questions. Was this the real River Styx? Had he always been the ferryman? Did he get time off?

Did I ask these questions? No.

Did I want to? So much. I had to fight to keep my lips zipped and not draw attention to myself.

Too bad, my silence wasn't helping me there at all.

One by one, each of the passengers turned to stare at me. They whispered to each other in tones too low for me to hear, but soon their voices got louder and louder.

"She's different."

"Look at her eyes."

"Her skin is so bright."

The fourth man didn't say anything, but he kept moving closer, inching toward me like I wouldn't notice.

"Umm, Charon?"

The ferryman ignored me, continuing to push off the bottom of the river with his pole, hurtling us forward over the water.

When the man got within touching distance, I noticed the sky beginning to roil, the scarlet clouds twisting and turning, growing darker with a coming storm. The sea beneath us began to churn, tossing the boat this way and that. The man was knocked away when a particularly nasty wave smacked into the skip.

Lightning crackled in the sky, the rumble of the following thunder shaking me to my bones.

"This is you, isn't it, child?"

I winced. "Probably? It happens on Earth a lot when I'm riled."

Charon—or rather, his hood—nodded.

The shadow of a giant serpent slithered through the water, its body circling the boat, bumping it a bit with every pass.

The silent man and his compatriots began moving toward me again, inching closer despite the crashing waves.

Fear cracked through me. I sure as shit didn't want to make a swim for it with that thing in the water, and Charon didn't seem too concerned that his passengers were eyeing me like a snack.

Lightning cracked again, casting shadows on the souls' faces. The boat rocked from the serpent bumping the hull once again.

And I didn't know which was worse.

The water.

Or the boat.

CHAPTER TWENTY-TWO

Thunder boomed at the same time lightning streaked across the sky. Only this time, it struck the man closest to me, blowing him off his feet and tossing him into the water. Before he could sink below the surface, the serpent raised his head from the depths and swallowed him whole.

It wasn't a snake, more like a fin-headed dragon with blue-green scales and horns that curled into spirals. I wanted to think it was pretty, and if it weren't the most terrifying fucking thing I'd seen in my entire life, I would have. If this was what the Loch Ness Monster was crafted after, I could see why so many people stayed out of the water.

The serpent followed the boat, catching up and keeping pace. If I didn't know better, it looked like a puppy waiting for me to drop more food. Its snout came closer and closer to the boat, sniffing at the passengers at the front. But the other souls seemed to see the error of attacking me, preferring to stay seated.

The sea dragon almost appeared to pout when we made it to shore, but that didn't stop it from coming closer, barring my exit to the dock even as the other souls tore out of the boat. Fear laced through me for one hot second, and then Charon began to chuckle.

"He likes you, child. He thinks you're pretty."

I didn't know how comforting that was, but I think I'd take that over him eating me. The sea dragon snuffled at me before doing almost the same thing Erebus had done, resting his jaw on my back like he was embracing me. Only, this dragon was enormous, and it was more like a wet full-body hug.

"Zillah, quit accosting my woman," Alistair griped from the shore, the reins of our two horses in his hand.

The dragon—Zillah—chuffed at Alistair, ignoring him completely. I patted the dragon's body, which given that it was so damn big, was all I could reach.

"One of my friends is half-dragon, and he isn't nearly as majestic and fearsome as you are."

Zillah let out a dragony purr as he pulled back. I got an up-close-and-personal view of his face. Blue-green scales faded to purple closer to his fins, but each one was iridescent like a fish. His eyes were a fantastic midnight blue that faded to an icy color close to his slit pupil. Those eyes were intelligent in a way I hadn't seen on many other animals. Erebus had that same intelligence—like he knew exactly what I was saying, and if I tried hard enough, I could understand him, too.

"I appreciate the assist back there. Sorry, you didn't get more snacks."

Zillah bowed his head in such a way, it looked like he was shrugging. It was an odd gesture on a dragon, but it made me smile. Alistair held out a hand from the dock, and I stepped off the boat, the earth shuddering under my feet.

"Is that normal? Please tell me the ground does that for everyone."

"No, love, that's just you."

Aces. "The souls in the boat did not give me the option of not saying anything to them, by the way. They kept talking about my eyes and my skin. Do I look different here or something?"

Alistair was leading me to the horses like I couldn't walk on my own. Funny, he'd been doing a lot of that. Keeping a hand on me while I was on the ground.

"Something is going on, Knight, and you're going to tell me what it is before I get angry."

He sighed, glancing back at me for a second until we reached the horses. "Get on the horse, and I'll tell you."

"You're only saying that because you know I can't kill

you while I'm on Erebus." Still, I got on the horse and absently started petting his neck to say my hellos.

"True," he said, mounting his own horse. "Your eyes glow, not with fire, but with magic. Your skin the same. And it did it before you crossed into Hell, so likely, Andras removed more than just a binder, he removed your glamour as well. The souls here can see you for what you are, a light, so they are drawn to you. It's why I've been a might bit more attentive than usual."

I huffed, wanting to be pissed at him, but just not able to scrounge up the energy for it.

"Fine. Just tell me next time, so I'm not blindsided by grabby hands, okay? So what's next on this plan of yours? Mine pretty much was get here. How to find Maria in this place is a little out of my wheelhouse. Unless I can use magic, but that might be a little dicey."

In a place where everything was amplified ten-fold with untested magic? Yeah, no thank you.

"We're headed to a market I know of. We've heard whispers that it has black market dealings. It might be where Selene was sold, and if so, they could know where Soren is. You up for that?"

The chance to fuck up a black-market dealer? Yes, please.

"Absolutely."

. . .

THE JOURNEY TO THE BLACK-MARKET DEALER was less than eventful. All I could see was desert, cracked, ruined earth, and the black mountain in the distance. There didn't seem to be a sun in Hell, just ambient light, so I couldn't tell how long we'd been here. The scarlet sky pushed in on us the deeper we traveled into the desert, and the mountain beyond never got any closer.

There also didn't seem to be a night, and I longed for a moon of some kind. I felt at home at night, anchored somehow, and here there wasn't anything to hold onto. I gripped Erebus' reins tighter in my fist just to find something to center myself.

Occasionally, we would pass souls stumbling toward the mountain, and I had to think this was also somehow a punishment. I wondered if the mountain beyond was an illusion, and I figured it probably was. After a few more hours of nothing, Alistair slowed his horse to a trot before stopping altogether. There wasn't a marker or anything to suggest this spot was different than any other patch of cracked dirt.

But Alistair climbed off his horse, anyway. Despite my misgivings, I followed suit. My ass numb from the trip, I stumbled a bit. The earth beneath me pitched and shook as if it didn't like me being here. Erebus snorted and stamped the ground, stepping in such a way that his body corralled me closer to the other horse. The pair of them hid me for lack of a better explanation, and I couldn't figure out why.

"Stay where you are, Max," Alistair called, his tone wary if not a little frightened. I couldn't see him to check if he was okay, the horses blocking my view.

I wanted to do what Alistair said, but something in me wouldn't allow him to get hurt because of me. Not again. I used Erebus' saddle as a footstool and propped myself up over his back to get a better look. Three substantial black dogs guarded a door that seemed to have sprung up out of nowhere. The door wasn't attached to anything but air, and even still, it wasn't what I would call remarkable. It looked like one of those hollow-core doors one would see in a shitty apartment, and it was dirty, covered in soot and grime.

The dogs themselves were about the size of a shifter-wolf, their eyes red as fresh-spilled blood, and their teeth as sharp as knives. They growled in unison as if they shared a brain. Maybe they did.

I made kissy noises at the beasts, and instantly, they quit growling at Alistair. I didn't know if they were shifters or if they were really dogs. I didn't know if they were like Erebus and Zillah or if they were mindless. But I was in the presence of puppies, and I wasn't going to be scared no matter how sharp their teeth were.

I stepped down from the stirrup and managed to skirt Erebus despite his best efforts. Now level with

Alistair, I knelt down on the ground, so I was face-to-face with the formerly snarling dogs.

"Hello, pretty puppies. I think we'd like to go through that door. Are you going to let us?"

Why I thought I could talk to Hell Hounds, I wasn't a hundred percent positive, but here I was.

The centermost dog sniffed at me before his tongue lolled out of his mouth. I let him sniff my hand, and he —or she, I couldn't be sure just yet—dipped his head under my hand for pets like any other dog would. The animals in this joint seemed to be super friendly. Soon, I had three noses in my face and was awash in doggy kisses. I gave as many pets as I could and a few scratches.

Did I turn into a fairytale princess when I wasn't looking?

"What in the bloody hell is with you and all the animals in this place?" Alistair broke in, wondering the same damn thing I was. "First it was Erebus, then Zillah, and now Hell Hounds? Really?"

Instead of answering him, I squealed when a particularly amorous hound licked me right in the ear.

"Okay, okay, okay, guys. Settle down." I got up off the ground, dusting off my leathers. "I'll give you more pats on the way out."

All three hounds sat down, but each one huffed as he did so.

Alistair snagged my hand, pulling me through the filthy door and into what looked like a tented bazaar. Stands filled with odds and ends littered the space. Each stand was unmanned, the trinkets dusty and unused. There was a still sort of silence to the place that didn't sit well with me. Not only had no one been here in a while, I had a feeling what we were seeing was a prop. No business was done in this place.

"Whatever you do, don't say anything, and please, for me, just look at the ground."

Alistair even pulled at the scarf I'd been using to keep dust from my mouth on the ride and pulled it over my hair like a hood.

"This isn't the place to be seen, love."

While I understood the wisdom in his words, I kind of wanted to punch him on general principle.

"Fine," I growled, petulant as fuck, but if it got my sister back, I'd do just about anything. Plus, eventually, I'd get to kick black marketeer ass.

He steeled himself and tightened his grip on my hand, picking his way through the rickety stands and narrow walkways. Eventually, we got to the front of the store—or maybe it was the back, considering how we entered.

Behind a particularly shabby counter, a behemoth of a man stood—if one could call this thing a man. With the face and head of a bull, the torso of a man, and a furred waist, I had no idea what this guy was. He didn't believe in shirts, either. He had hoops through his ears, nose, and nipples, and golden rings on every finger.

Alistair moved his hand like he wanted me to stand behind him, but the part of me that wanted to kick him for thinking I was the kind of woman who would allow that, only made me move slightly instead of completely behind him. Yes, that minotaur-looking motherfucker could see me, but he wasn't really looking at me.

No, his gaze was fixed on the Knight, and as he recognized him, he gave Alistair a toothy grin.

"Alistair Quinn, long time no see. Come to barter? Or maybe with the woman you're trying to hide, you've come here to sell."

Alistair shook his head, his voice just shy of a growl when he answered him. "Neither, Taurus. I've come for information."

Taurus gave him a smarmy smile. "Sorry, I'm not dealing in information today. Come back tomorrow, and we'll see."

Fucker.

"That doesn't work for me, Taurus. I want to know where my father is, and I want to know now."

Taurus chuckled darkly. "Too bad, I don't give a shit what you wa—"

Abruptly, Taurus stopped talking, taking in a huge

sniff, scenting the air like he caught a whiff of something tasty.

Dred yawned wide in my belly, and I had to force myself not to take a step back. That plan went to shit almost as soon as I thought it, because Taurus was up and over the counter, knocking Alistair away with a flick of his hand. I flew with him, landing on a pile of junk.

The shattered edge of something sharp dug into the side of my cheek and the palm of my hand, spilling my blood on the ground. I struggled to stand, shock from the landing making me woozy. All too soon, my feet left the earth as a beefy hand yanked me up by my leathers. Giant hands turned me until I was face-to-face with Taurus.

Up close, he was scarier than he had been on the other side of the counter. His teeth were filed flat like a horse, but their edges seemed sharp, cutting. As he brought his face closer to me, I tried to struggle, but he was just too big. Taurus sniffed at me once, twice, before he snaked out a tongue and licked my cheek.

Oh, fucking gross.

"Who are you, and what are you doing in my market?"

Instead of answering him, I was distracted by Alistair coming at him with his scythe ready to strike. Taurus tucked me close and knocked Alistair away like he'd flicked a bug off his shoulder.

Alistair went flying again, and I had no choice but to answer him.

"I—I'm Max. Daughter of Andras and grand-daughter of Lilith." I figured name dropping was okay, just this once if it meant this huge fucker would let me go.

Taurus chuckled mirthlessly, shaking his head. "You lie. I have tasted your blood, child, and you do not belong to either of them. No, you smell and taste of Fae."

I shook my head. "I'm not. My parents are Teresa Alcado and the demon Andras."

Taurus looked at me thoughtfully.

"That might be what they told you, child, but you aren't anything but Fae blood. I've tasted many of your kind, and you taste just like them." He said it like Fae blood was a favorite dish he missed because the restaurant had gone out of business.

Fae. There was no way. Taurus had to be lying, or mistaken, or... he was telling the truth, and everyone had lied to me.

My mother. My father. Bernadette. Caim. All of them. I didn't come up with the demon idea on my own. No, I'd been told I was a demon.

I wanted to believe the people closest to me wouldn't lie about something like that, but with their history of deceit, I just couldn't put it past them.

"I bet I'll fetch a pretty penny selling you," he purred in my ear, snuffling at my neck.

I shuddered, struggling to get out of his monster-sized hands. I couldn't reach my weapons, and Taurus was holding me so tight, I couldn't feel my fingers enough to snap them.

The growl coming from Alistair's throat practically vibrated in the space. "You will let her go, Taurus."

"Or what, Knight? Are you going to try to fight me? You won't win, and you know it."

"She is my wife," Alistair insisted, his voice a growl or warning.

Taurus huffed. "I smell no bond on her. She belongs to no one."

I met Alistair's gaze over Taurus' beefy shoulder.

"Remember that favor you owe me, love? I think I'm going to have to call it in."

CHAPTER TWENTY-THREE

H e was bringing up that favor shit *now*?

"Are you fucking kidding me with that shit?"

Taurus, to his credit, bellowed out a laugh at my objection.

I didn't mean to protest quite so vehemently. Honestly, it just slipped out. But come the fuck on. *Wife*? I was no one's wife or wife material by any stretch of the imagination.

"Becoming my wife isn't the favor. Asking questions about this particular facet of our relationship is. *Trust* me, love. That's the favor. No questions, just do it."

Taurus took that opportunity to lick at the blood running down my cheek. It was either marry Alistair right this fucking second or deal with being sold. Or eaten.

Wild-eyed, I frantically nodded.

"Do you take me as yours?" Alistair asked.

"Yes," I croaked, and he sighed in relief before mouthing what I was supposed to say.

I sucked in a huge breath, steeling myself for something I couldn't name. Yes, I was being held against a wall by a minotaur. Yes, this was not how I'd planned this day to go, but still...

"Alistair, do you take me as your wife?"

"Yes, love." He seemed almost proud to say those words, and I supposed that went a little way toward making up for the ambush wife bullshit. Not a lot, but if it meant we got out of this, I was probably going to forgive him.

Someday.

"Fine. You've bound her. I hope you're happy." Taurus grumbled like Alistair had taken his favorite toy. Then, he dropped me like a sack of moldy potatoes.

I crumpled to the cracked earth, unable to stop myself from smacking face-first on the ground because my arms were numb from Taurus' hold. Alistair rushed to me, helping me up. Slicing his thumb with a fang, he ran the bloody digit over my wounds.

I couldn't figure out why he would do that when they would heal soon, anyway.

"We need to clean up your blood, love. The last thing we need is for another demon to smell it." He snatched a tablecloth from one of the stands and started rubbing at the blood on my face.

My breath whooshed out of me.

"Did you know?" I croaked, hurt lacing the question.

"No, Max. I would never keep that from you. Not ever." Alistair's phased golden gaze met mine, and I knew he was telling the truth.

"Aww, young love," Taurus trilled, sarcastically batting his bull eyelashes at us.

The fucker.

"Hey, Taurus," I called. "Want to see what a pissed off Fae can do?"

Without thought or a plan of any kind, I snapped the fingers of my left hand, binding his arms and legs with invisible restraints. The thunder that I'd wished for cracked outside the bazaar tent, the lightning flashing through the thick fabric.

"I'm not sure what my powers will do here, but I'm very interested in finding out. Aren't you? Now, I want some information. Since you aren't dealing in information today, I suppose I'll just have to figure out a way to entertain myself until you're inclined to give me what I want. Now, we're in Hell, so fire would be appropriate, but it feels too overdone. Hmmm."

I tapped my bloody fingers against my mouth, uncaring that Alistair had just scrubbed my face clean.

"Let me go, you fairy bitch. There's nothing you can do to me to make me talk. I've survived eons, and I'll continue on living after you're dust," Taurus spat, baring his teeth at me.

"You know, you're probably right," I murmured, my words like a threat.

I clapped my bloody hand to the side of his head, drilling into his mind to unearth everything I wanted to know.

Taurus was business savvy, plucking wayward souls like seashells. Every time he found a pretty one, he stole it. For the damned souls, that wasn't an issue. In fact, that was his actual job. No, the problem came when he found shiny souls that weren't damned at all. Demons, Fae traversing the realm, dragons, and the like. Shoving them in cages and selling them off to the highest bidder.

And typically, the highest bidder was Soren mother-fucking Quinn.

Taurus delivered the souls personally to a place he called the Seam—the nothingness between Hell and Faerie.

I pulled out of Taurus' head and asked the question I knew he would answer. "Where is the Seam?"

Sure, Taurus' eyes, nose, and ears were bleeding, and

Alistair was struggling to hold him up, but I was going to get answers.

One way or the other.

"P-past the mountain. Short—there's a shortcut in the back room. Too hard to take all those souls the long way," he answered, and I narrowed my eyes.

"Very good. Any traps I should be aware of?" Alistair asked. "Is he expecting a shipment?"

Taurus coughed, his blood spraying the air, but I managed to move out of the way before I got sullied.

"No and no. And it won't matter. What he's doing can't be stopped. Not by you, and surely not by this fairy bitch. What did he take from you, may I ask, to make you this stupid?"

I was sure my smile was feral, because even though his sight was slightly obscured with blood, he still flinched when I answered him.

"My sister."

As it turned out, there were several "shortcuts" in Taurus' back room. There were hundreds of doors back there. Some no bigger than crawlspaces, some so ornate, they had to go back to the human realm. And some, just like I thought, were black as night, and nearly impossible to see without eyes like mine.

Fae eyes.

Hadn't Barrett said something about my sight recently? How it was odd I could see magic? If I was a Fae—and I wasn't saying I was—it was possible that it made a whole hell of a lot of sense. I could see and smell magic when no one else could. I could draw power from myself rather than the earth or the moon. I could conjure from nothing…

I shook myself.

No.

I was the daughter of Teresa and Andras.

I was the granddaughter of Bernadette.

I was *not* a Fae, and the fact that I could see this door meant I was a special kind of demon.

Luckily, I'd decided keeping Taurus alive was a better plan than what I really wanted to do to him. That was to set the Hounds on him and see how long it took for them to get full. I was sure they would enjoy their feast, but that would have to wait until we returned with Maria.

Before we left, I made sure Taurus was secured, hogtying him with vines conjured from nothing. Vines that had poisoned barbs every few inches should he decide trying to escape was a good idea. Taurus wasn't too happy with me, but I had more than a few plans for him. The fact that he couldn't die, just made them all the more fun.

I studied the door that led to the Seam, unable to make myself just open it and file in. Yes, my sister was on the other side, but I knew better than anyone that just because I wanted to be able to get through this, I probably wouldn't.

"I need you to do something for me, okay?"

Something about my tone gave Alistair pause, and he snatched up my hand, yanking me around to face him.

"I don't know what you're about to say, but please, love, please don't. What did you say? 'I didn't just get you for you to sign your own death warrant now.'"

Regret washed over me. Regret that I wouldn't get a happy ending with Alistair. That I wouldn't get to tell my family I loved them one last time.

I pulled out a special jar I crafted from the ashes of my burning tree and my blood. It was fortified to hold precisely one soul. It was how I planned on returning her to our plane and past the walls. I knew all too well that there was no other way to bring her back.

Putting the jar in his hand, I closed his fingers around it.

"If for whatever reason I don't make it, this is how you take Maria back. And here are my coins for the ferry if you need them for her. I'm trusting you with this, Alistair. I'm trusting you just like you asked me to. If I don't make it, bring her back for me, okay?"

Alistair pressed his lips together like if he didn't,

he'd scream at me. He looked like he wanted to smack the jar and coins out of our joined hands. Like he wanted to smash them to bits because if he had to use them, it meant…

"You're coming back with me," he insisted. "You are. There is no other option. Do you hear me, Maxima? I will pull you from the depths if I have to."

Then his lips were on mine, a fierce, hard kiss that made me feel like he was branding me with something I couldn't name.

"You're coming back with me," he whispered again against my lips. "No matter what. I didn't just find you after all these years to lose you now."

"Still. Hold onto them for me?" I murmured, my voice breaking as I looked into those golden eyes of his phased form. The charred, burning skin was starting to grow on me.

"I will, but only because you'll be getting them back. Understand?"

I only smiled.

I knew better than to make promises I couldn't keep.

In the end, it took both of us to open the door to the Seam. The doorknob felt like burning ice, and as I held it, it seemed to drain the very marrow from my bones. Stumbling back, I whirled, marching over to Taurus.

"Did you leave something out, you fuck? How am I supposed to open that door?"

Taurus' eyes held a malicious gleam, and I knew he wasn't going to answer me. Not without an incentive. My smile was feral as I clenched my fists in front of his face and watched his eyes bulge as the poison vines tightened around his body.

"F-fine! I'll tell you," he gasped.

I loosened his bonds only slightly as I waited for an answer to my question. He had five seconds to start talking, or I was going to make sure every thorn in those vines made their way into his flesh.

Five. Four. Three…

"It takes two. Usually, I use up one of the souls on the way, but if you want to live, it will take the both of you."

I didn't trust Taurus, but we were running out of time. We reached for the doorknob, and the metal siphoned magic from us faster than I thought possible. The two seconds it took to open the door felt like years.

Once the door cracked, we tossed it open together. The opening revealed a midnight path of cobblestones that were probably less stone and more bones and body parts. Beyond the path laid another door, only this one was ten-stories tall and at least fifty-feet wide. The arch of the entrance was an ornate stone carving of bodies in agony and devils torturing them with pitchforks.

It looked like the gate to Tartarus rather than the Seam.

And we were about to go through it.

CHAPTER TWENTY-FOUR

There was no way to stealthily open a fifty-foot-wide door. While I could most definitely snap my way into that room or castle or pit, it seemed like a horrible idea—even for me. The best I could do was see if my magic would let us pass through the damn thing without opening it.

I rifled through my pouch of goodies, hoping I was smart enough to bring chalk. When I finally located the bit of white underneath a shit-ton of vials, I breathed a small sigh of relief.

There was likely no way to go in there unnoticed, but I had to try something.

The chalk glided over the ornately carved door like butter, and as soon as I completed the drawing, the outer edges of it began to glow green. At first, I thought maybe the spell didn't work, but what I didn't realize right away was that the other side of the door was pure blackness. Uncertain, I held up a hand to see if it could pass through unimpeded. When my fingers drifted past the surface, I hazarded a guess that passing through this blackness was about all we were going to get.

Drawing back, I turned to Alistair, pricking my thumb with one of my athames and brushing the blood down the center of his forehead to the tip of his nose. *Ick*, but necessary as I copied a blessing my mother had given me what seemed like too long ago.

Alistair needed to be blessed before he followed me through that door. Staring into his eyes, I gave him what I could.

"I bless you with all that I am, and all that I will be. May you have safety on your travels. May your aim always be true. May you see what others cannot. May your victories far outweigh your losses. May your losses teach you, and may your love guide you."

I knew when my mother blessed me this way, she'd never expected to see me again. And now that those same words fell from my lips, I understood them for what they were. They were a wish for safety and security. A wish for someone you loved to keep breathing when you thought you might not.

There was more I wanted to say to him, more I wanted to experience with him, but we just didn't have the time.

Alistair pricked his thumb on his fangs and pressed it into the pad of mine to heal the cut, and all of a sudden, his eyes widened. His gaze passed over the door and the surrounding structure.

"Is this what you see all the time?" he whispered.

I nodded. "Don't get used to it, the sight will fade soon enough."

Together we approached the door once more, tentatively testing our hands with the barrier. When we felt no resistance, Alistair passed through first, and I followed. The ground beneath my feet seemed almost buoyant, like gravity was lax here. As my eyes adjusted to the darkness, I could faintly make out impossibly high arches and wall carvings, like we were stepping into a palace of some kind.

Maybe it had been once, but it felt almost abandoned now. And I said almost because I could feel the disturbance on the air of people—or souls, or demons, or things—moving around us. I couldn't see them yet, but they were out there. I wondered if it was good or very bad that I couldn't hear the screaming I'd heard both times I'd entered Maria's mind.

My gut went with bad.

I squeezed Alistair's hand, and we moved forward into the dark castle, stepping carefully as we traversed deeper into the blackness. I began to worry more when I realized a little too late that the fire under his skin couldn't pierce the darkness surrounding us. Even the runes carved into his flesh barely shone.

It was then that a man's hand closed around my throat, cutting off my air and ripping me away from Alistair.

"Max!" Alistair bellowed, his arms outstretched to find me in the dark, but I couldn't answer him.

Before I knew what was happening—okay, I knew I was caught, but still—or who had me, my body hit the wonky floor. I could barely see in this place, but I knew who had me, at least. A demon with shining eyes stood tall, looming over me like the god he thought he was.

Soren Quinn. It had to be. Phased he looked just like his son, charred skin, barely glowing runes and all. Only, his eyes were very different. Alistair's glowed with the fire of his demon. Soren's eyes were all black but still seemed to shine with magic.

My arms and legs brushed barely warm limbs of women huddled together in this dark place, and I wanted to search them for Maria. I did.

But I couldn't tear my gaze from Soren's. His smile seemed so smug, like he had a plan and I'd played right into it.

"Maxima Alcado. It's good to see you. I thought you'd never get here. Can I call you Max? Or should I call you by the name you were born with? Massima Bertrand Laffitte. The last living Elemental Fae in all nine realms. Do you know how long it took to track you down?"

I was still stuck on the bullshit name he called me. *Massima?* What kind of name was that? And *Elemental Fae?* Was there even such a thing?

Soren didn't like my silence and he reached down to close his hand around my throat again, picking me up off the ground like I weighed nothing. He shook me a little, bringing my face closer to his. He could see perfectly fine in the dim, and I realized all too quickly there was no way he was born with those eyes.

No, he'd stolen them. Probably from a Fae who could see in this place better than I ever could.

"*Detrahet me in lucem,*" I breathed with my last bit of air, snapping my fingers on both hands.

Light bloomed in my hands for barely a second before it fizzled away to nothing. He roared, the light searing his eyes for a few precious moments. The light was gone, but it was enough to get him to let me go, and that's all I'd really been after.

Scrambling backward, I quickly ran back into the cold bodies on the floor, the women shivering as they huddled together.

"Max?" a woman croaked, reaching for me with a weak hand. I grabbed at it as she searched in the dark for me. *Maria.*

I pulled her into a swift hug, and then I recognized

the emaciated woman right next to her. *Lachesis*. Or rather, her soul.

Soren had stolen the soul of a goddess. A Fate.

I'd just made that realization before I was hauled up and away, flying through the air only to slam into a very solid wall, my skull knocking against the stone.

"You think one silly light spell is going to stop me? You stupid girl. Did you really think I didn't move all the chess pieces myself just to get you here?"

It made sense in a diabolical, evil mastermind kind of way. But I didn't know the details and I needed to stall him long enough for Alistair to find us.

"I kinda hoped you were just working on blind luck and a can-do attitude. Silly me."

Was it smart to antagonize the super demon? Probably not. Especially with blood running into my eyes.

"Your weakness is and always has been your family. Your parents, your sister, your friends. They weaken you. Make you stupid. I knew if I took your sister, you'd come right where I needed you. And I was right."

"What other chess pieces did you move? Besides Elias, Deya, your wife, the attack on Aether, Cinder's brainwashing... Am I missing anything?"

I groaned as I tried to get my feet under me.

"Oh, wait, aren't you stealing the magic from the gate?" I added and watched with satisfaction as his eerie eyes went wide.

"So you aren't as stupid as I thought. I wonder if you've put together *why* I want you here."

"I gotta say, Soren, that I don't know. I know we're in the Seam, but other than that." I shrugged by way of answer.

I managed to stand, my balance completely fucked from the wonky floor and head injury.

"You're right we are in the Seam—the Seam between Hell and Faerie. Right now, it's a black void, a gate that lets no one through. But soon, it will be open, and you are the last Fae who can open it. Your parents thought they could hide what you are from me. Like I didn't strike that bargain with Abaddon because of what you are."

That didn't make any sense and I told him so. "You made that bargain before I was ever born."

"As if your Lilith is the only seer who can predict what's to come. I knew the daughter of Andras was going to be the key. I just didn't know you would be his adopted daughter. Then there was that mess with Abaddon, and I knew... I knew it was you. He killed his own father to keep you safe from me. As if killing him would stop the agreement. What really pissed me off was all the men I've sent to take you to me ended up dead right alongside him. That's when I knew I'd have to make you come to me."

And I had. I'd walked right into this fucked up castle

and played right into his hands.

Faintly, I could see a figure standing at the archway between this room and the other. I wasn't sure if it was the entryway we'd come through, but it could be. The figure took small, measured steps toward the women huddling on the ground.

Alistair.

He needed to move faster. If Soren caught Alistair, he'd likely toss him into the void right along with me. And that was what Soren was saying, right? He wanted to open the gate, so sacrifice the last person to be able to do it. It was standard operating procedure for evil villains everywhere.

"Well, I guess you've won, then. Want to tell me why you want to open the door to a realm you've never even fucking seen, let alone could possibly be a big fish in? Tell me, how does that work? Is it a grass is greener situation, or are you just an idiot?"

Yes, I was taunting him, but I needed his eyes on me and not Alistair stealing back the souls that didn't belong here.

But Soren was too smart for that.

"Hello, *son*," he called before he flashed from in front of me and behind his son.

His fingers grabbed hold of Alistair's hair and Soren whipped him into the closest pillar, cracking the stone with a hiss. Soren wasn't done with him, though, because he picked Alistair up like a rag doll and slammed him into the ground over and over again.

White-hot anger surged through me, and without a thought, I snapped my fingers. I had no idea what my magic was supposed to do, but lightning arced through the room, a bolt shooting from my fingertips and knocking into Soren's chest. Soren flew off his feet, smacking into the wobbly ground.

I staggered toward the women and Alistair, falling to a crawl when my legs refused to hold me up.

"Maria," I croaked, "baby sister, we've got to get out of here. Can any of you walk? If so, you need to get up right now."

Using the last bit of strength I had, I performed a spell I'd been unable to do before.

"*Sanitatem*," I muttered, breathing health into my baby sister's soul. She had to make it. She had to.

"Get up, baby sister. Get the others. Get out of here."

With fumbling fingers, I clumsily yanked an athame from its sheath. Soren wasn't going to stay down. Not with all the power he'd adsorbed. He needed to die, and now.

"Max, what are you doing?" she asked.

I didn't rightly know. All I knew was Soren had to die. How I was going to accomplish that was a mystery.

"Killing the boogeyman, sweetheart. Like I've always done."

I had no illusions that cutting off the serpent's head was going to do any good. But I figured if that wouldn't kill him, it sure as hell would drain him of power. Maybe if I tapped his jugular like a keg, all that magic would come slipping out.

Only one way to find out.

CHAPTER TWENTY-FIVE

S tanding was a bitch. A cold-hearted, miserable bitch. What little I could see of the room pitched, and I stumbled, nearly dropping my athame.

If I was going to do this, and by this, I meant cutting off Soren's head, then I needed to get my shit together. Steadying myself, I got within touching distance before he began to rouse. One would think a lightning bolt to the sternum would be enough to buy a gal some time, but nooooooo.

I was stuck with Soren the super demon and his plan for realm domination.

I didn't have the strength to lift the blade above my head, but I did have enough juice left in my limbs to stab the shit out of his belly. So that's what I did.

Problem was, that little "poke" with my blade seemed to rouse him faster than anything I'd ever seen.

Okay, so I didn't "poke" him. I may have extended the blade on my athame and slashed his belly from hip to hip. One would assume that gutting a demon would offer her a little bit of dying.

Not so much.

Not a second later, Soren was on me, slashing at my fragile skin with abandon, his talons ripping into me like tissue paper.

Alistair charged him, knocking Soren off of me, but he fared no better than I did. Soren quickly got the upper hand, wrenching his son from him and tossing him away as if he weighed nothing. And then he was on me again.

"You will open this gate, Maxima, or I swear you will watch as I murder every single person you hold dear."

His talons squeezed my throat, as his stolen Fae eyes blazed with a magic I couldn't name. Unfortunately, I couldn't help but believe him.

"What will happen if I open it?"

"Does it matter?"

Did it? Yes. It did. If it meant Hell on Earth, if it meant millions of deaths, if it meant the end of us, then yes, it mattered.

"Yes." I seethed, putting as much venom as I could into that little, insignificant word.

"With your death, the wall between Hell and Faerie will fade away. Demons won't be beholden to our charges. We won't be forced to this life of servitude. Pigeonholed into a second-class citizenship because we punish the wicked. We will be free."

When he put it like that, I could see why he'd want to open the gate. Too bad I could smell the lie on him. It smelled sickly sweet on the stale air, and I knew he wanted more than freedom.

"Let Alistair, Maria, and Lachesis go. You let them go and I'll open the gate."

"Max," Alistair growled, "don't do this."

I could just make out Soren's smile, it was all fangs and falsehoods. He was getting what he wanted, why shouldn't he smile?

"If that is your bargain, I will accept. I will let them go."

That didn't mean he wouldn't find them again once this was all over.

"You let them go forever, Soren. You don't look for them, you don't have anyone look for them. You forget their names and faces. You forget they exist."

His smile was almost proud that I'd thought to cover my ass. "Of course, if that is what you wish, I will honor it."

"No, Max. He won't hold up his end," Maria insisted. "He'll kill us the first chance he gets."

I was counting on that.

What was the lore on fairy deals? If you made one, you'd better keep it, or your life would be forfeit. If I was a Fae, then he'd die the second he broke our deal.

"It's fine, Maria," I said trying to soothe her. "It'll be okay."

I might be dying in this deal, but I was taking him with me.

"Let me hug them one last time, and you'll have what you want."

Soren sneered at my request but set me down. "Foolish sentiment."

I staggered, barely holding myself up, but Maria caught me. Her soul was so strong. I'd gone into this knowing I wouldn't come back out of it. I just wanted one more hug. One more squeeze. One more chance to tell her all the things I couldn't before.

"You're going to make it, baby girl. You're going to go back and hug Mom and make babies and live an extraordinary life. That's all I ever wanted for you since the day you were born. So you do it, okay?"

"Not without you," she sobbed. "There hasn't been a time in my life that you haven't been there in the back of my mind. Driving me to question everything. Pushing me to make better choices. What kind of life am I going to have without you in it?"

"It doesn't matter, sweet girl. You'll have one, and

that's what matters." I kissed her on the forehead, gave her one last hug, and stood on my own, swiping my tears away.

I moved to Lachesis, the soul of the Fate, haggard and far too thin. Soren had drained her, used her, and left her to rot.

"Tell your sisters I tried, okay? I didn't mean to fail them."

Lachesis' eyes gained a small spark of life. "I know, Maxima. It'll be all right."

I hoped she was right.

When I reached Alistair, he refused to look at me.

"You were supposed to come back with me, Max." He seethed, so mad that this was how it was going down, he could spit nails.

I'd tried to tell him, but he was so determined to be right, he didn't see that there was no way he'd get what he wanted.

"Come on, Knight, kiss me goodbye," I teased, even though my eyes were filling again, and my voice broke. "Please? I can do this if you're going to live. So kiss me goodbye and take care of my sister, okay?"

Alistair grabbed me, clutching me to his chest as if he never wanted to let me go. In turn, I cupped his face in my hands and kissed him with all the things I would never get a chance to say. When it ended, it felt too brief, not big enough for all the kisses we'd miss. But

Soren wouldn't wait forever, and I had to make sure my people were taken care of.

Soren smiled when I started toward him. He reached for a piece of fabric I hadn't noticed with all the 'being tossed around' shenanigans. The fabric covered most of a wall, and when it was torn away, all I could see was a gilt-framed opening and the blackness beyond it. The nothingness appeared like pictures of black holes, the beauty of stars around a pit so deep nothing could escape it.

It probably wasn't the worst way to go. Out of all the times I'd died, it would probably even be peaceful. A sigh of resignation fell from my lips.

Four hundred years. Gone in a blink.

Without warning, Maria let out a screeching howl of rage, streaking across the room toward Soren with one of my athames in her hand. She'd extended the blade, turning it into a sword, and she wasn't stopping. She went right for him, ducking at the last second and shoving the blade through his middle to the hilt.

With a quick flick of her wrist, she brought the blade up, slicing toward his sternum.

Then everything seemed to slow down to fractions of a second that I only saw in flashes. Flashes of memories that would haunt me until the day I died.

Maria's vicious smile of triumph when she caught Soren by surprise.

Her dainty foot coming up to push him off the blade. Her pride at saving me for once.

Soren's shock as he fell backward toward the framed void.

His finger scrabbling at air until he caught Maria's wrist.

Maria losing her grip on the blade.

Maria falling with Soren into the nothingness.

We tried to reach her. Or at least I did.

But I wasn't fast enough.

CHAPTER TWENTY-SIX

I'd failed at a lot of things in my life. I failed at being a witch, at being a good daughter, at being anything but a blight on the universe. I couldn't recall a single thing I'd succeeded at in my long life that hadn't cost me more than I was willing to pay.

After Maria fell, I'd tried to get her, tried to reach for her. But I couldn't get close enough, fast enough. I'd been too late, and then Alistair hauled me away with his arm around my middle as I screamed for my sister.

Watching her fall.

I screamed for a long time, long after we made it out of the dark castle and back to the bazaar.

I tried bargaining. I tried threatening. But nothing I said made Alistair take me back to that castle. Alistair took every hit, every insult, every mean thing I could think of, and ignored it so he could haul me out of Hell kicking and screaming.

I petered out somewhere in the middle of the desert, but that didn't stop the tears. Alistair's way out of the realm was much faster than our way in, or maybe it seemed that way because I wasn't too lucid.

He held me close to his chest as we shared Erebus' saddle, leaving the other horse for Lachesis. But these details filtered into my brain slowly, as if it took my brain far too long to process the fact that there was no going back.

I wasn't exactly sure how we got home, or how I made it from Hell to Aether to my bed.

Did it matter? Not really.

I didn't recall falling asleep on the trip, but I must have, right?

The tears stopped around day two, but that didn't stop me from staring off into space as I tried to wrap my brain around the fact that she wasn't here.

In fact, no one was here except Aidan, Della, and Alistair. Everyone kept a wide berth except Alistair. He made sure I ate, that I slept, that I sat up every once in a while. I couldn't say what my other friends did. I vaguely remembered them being here when we made it back, but when they realized we came back alone…

I wanted to care for their loss as well, but I just couldn't let my heart bend to another person's pain.

Not Teresa's, not Ian's. I couldn't care about them, or what was happening with Cinder, or where Striker was, or what would happen with Selene.

I wanted to be big enough to handle it—*them*—but I wasn't.

It wasn't until day three that Aidan made me go downstairs to eat. I sipped at soup and nibbled on crackers, but even I knew I was wasting away. I couldn't drum up enough emotion to care.

Numbness was my friend. If I stayed numb, then I could breathe a little. I couldn't even think her name anymore, that's how much it hurt. But I couldn't force myself to forget her, that was like drinking poison.

"Being your paladin is the worst job ever," Aidan griped, the first I'd heard anyone speak in days. Already I was missing the silence.

"Sorry you feel that way," I replied.

"If it isn't you trying to get yourself killed, it's you trying to save people who can't be saved. Or pissing off beings so out of your league, it's a miracle you're even still breathing. Corax, and Princes of Hell, and suped-up moon witches with axes to grind. Don't you care that your grandmother has a penchant for setting people on fire? And if you die, *I* would be next. Do you care? No, you don't."

"She's not really my grandmother, you know."

Aidan scoffed. "Just because you're adopted doesn't mean they aren't your family."

I huffed out a laugh. It was pitiful at best, but it was what I had.

"Bernadette lied to me, didn't she? She made you my paladin long before I killed Samael. You might not have hated me, but you wanted me out of your life. You tolerated me and then... you just pulled a one-eighty. What did she say to you to make you choose this job?"

Aidan stared at the carpet, his whiskey glass held loosely in his fingers as they dangled between his knees.

"She could see you needed help—"

"Don't lie to me. My father thought you were my mate because of the way you protected me, but I know better than anyone that you don't have those kinds of feelings for me. What did she say to you to change your mind?"

"She told me that if I didn't get my head out of my ass—or *arse* as she put it—that you'd get killed. That your blood would be on my hands because of my indifference. That I'd put my life on the line for my brother when he wasn't the one who needed saving. That I was meant for more than just saving Ian all the time. That you were more important than a promise I made a century ago."

"What promise did you make?"

"You know my scars?" he said gesturing to his forehead, to the puckered skin I knew was hidden under his beanie. "I got them for Ian. To get him free. His mother did that to me. It was my sacrifice to get him away from her. You know her. Her name is Deya Baptiste. I swore to her that I would protect her son. Swore that I would keep him from our father, and I have. But now I know that Ian never needed my help at all."

If Deya was the goddess she said she was, and Ian was her son, then no, he never needed his brother's help. Not even a little.

"But when I made my paladin oath, I didn't know what I know now. That you were as important as you are. But Bernadette is mighty convincing, and I made it because I needed more than just being a big brother. I needed more than just looking after him. I needed to be worth more than that."

"What will you do now?" I wondered aloud.

"My job, Max. The way you're glowing now, I need to hang around for a while."

That brought a smile to my face.

But it didn't last.

ANGER CAME AT DAY FIVE.

They said there were five stages of grief: denial, anger, bargaining, depression, and acceptance. What they didn't say was that these stages could be felt simultaneously or out of order. Denial came first, but that only lasted for about a millisecond. Depression came next, and with it all the numbness that protected me. Bargaining was on a constant loop.

What if I'd have moved faster? What if she would have just let me save her? Was she really gone? And my personal favorite: *If I opened that gate, would she come out on the other side?*

Those thoughts were always there. Cutting at me every single second I was awake.

Anger came next, and the people in my life were feeling all the wrath I could muster and then some. Every stick of furniture in my living room was in shambles, the drywall scorched and cracked, the ceiling molding ripped from the plaster.

Nothing was safe.

Alistair tried to talk me down, but I couldn't quite look at him without losing it. I had a feeling he brought in Della because he knew I couldn't—or wouldn't—hurt her.

"You have to knock this shit off, Max," she said as she held a chair to fend me off like a lion tamer.

"Why? Why should I stop? I destroy everything I touch. I get people I love killed," I snarled, ripping a bookcase from the wall and watching as it smashed onto the hardwood floors. "Why shouldn't I rip everything I have apart?"

Della's tears didn't help my anger, it just made me madder, made me want to snap my fingers and destroy everything I could reach.

"I couldn't save Melody." *Smash*. "I couldn't save Maria." *Rip*. "All I do is kill and destroy, Della. Why shouldn't I rip this whole fucking place apart? Huh?"

Yes, I was screaming at the top of my lungs, hadn't showered in who knew when, and was in the middle of a living room's worth of rubble.

But what I said was still true.

I'd failed at everything. *Everything...*

I didn't realize I'd said those words aloud until Della contradicted me.

"You have not failed, Max. You went to Hell to save a soul that couldn't be saved. Maria died, sweetheart. She died and Soren stole her. She didn't belong in Hell, and she doesn't belong in that abyss, but you didn't do anything wrong."

That was all well and good, but I knew better.

"And Melody..." She trailed off, tearing a hand through her chestnut hair. "I wasn't here for that, but I know you did all you could. In fact, I have some news if you want to calm yourself down enough to hear it."

I eyed her warily, but I wasn't screaming or throwing things, so that was as calm as she was going to get.

"Remember that incubus that came to Aether? The one that wanted to talk to Striker?"

I carefully stepped out of a pile of rubble, wanting to be on solid ground for whatever she had to tell me.

"Yeah," I hedged.

"He has a problem. His parents adopted an infant. An incubus without a mother. A few days ago, the mother they thought was dead, came to their home looking for her son. A son she named Ronan."

I felt dizzy for a second, and I reached for the closest wall that was still sturdy enough to hold me up.

"She took him, the boy's mother, in the night while they were sleeping. Took him right out of his crib. But she left a note. Want to guess what it said?"

"Tell me," I ordered.

"It said that she'd taken him home with her. To Faerie."

Melody was alive.

I hadn't failed them all.

I hadn't failed her.

I was grasping all of this when Della asked her next question, one that hit me like a ton of bricks and buoyed me more than anything else ever could.

"So when are we leaving?"

Max's story will continue with…
Priestess of Storms & Stone
Rogue Ethereal Book Five

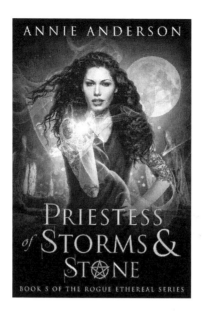

PRIESTESS OF STORMS & STONE
Rogue Ethereal Book Five

If there is one lesson I've been taught in my life, it's that fairies are the absolute worst.

Finding a fledgling succubus in Faerie is like locating a needle inside a realm-sized haystack. With a guide I can't trust and a goal more ephemeral than smoke, my odds of success are tenuous at best. Not to mention, as the last Elemental in existence, I have a giant target painted on my back.

Because one half of Faerie wants me dead, and the other half wants to use me as a sacrifice to open the gates to

Earth. But I swore I would find my quarry, and I will. Even if I have to rip the entire realm apart to do it.

There is a storm coming to Faerie. And that storm is me.

-Preorder now on Amazon-
Coming March 31, 2020

THE PHOENIX RISING SERIES

an adult paranormal romance series by Annie Anderson

Heaven, Hell, and everything in between. Fall into the realm of Phoenixes and Wraiths who guard the gates of the beyond. That is, if they can survive that long…

Living forever isn't all it's cracked up to be.

Check out the Phoenix Rising Series today!

THE SHELTER ME SERIES

a Romantic Suspense series by Annie Anderson

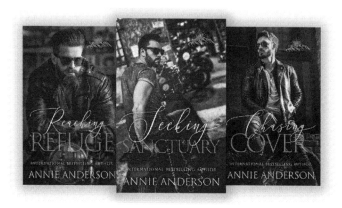

A girl on the run. A small town with a big secret.
Some sanctuaries aren't as safe as they appear...

Planning to escape her controlling boyfriend, Isla's getaway hits a snag when a pair of pink lines show up on a pregnancy test.

Levi just needs an accountant. Someone smart, dependable, and someone who won't blow town and leave him in the lurch. When a pretty but battered woman falls into his arms, he can't help but offer her the job. If only he can convince her to take it.

As an unexpected death rocks this small Colorado town, Isla can't help but wonder if her past somehow followed her to the one place she's felt at home.

Check out the Shelter Me Series today!

SEEK YOU FIND ME

A Romantic Suspense Newsletter Serial

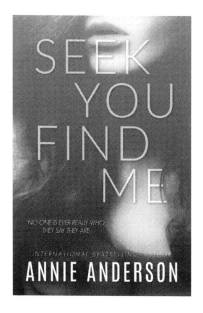

Never fall in love with your mark.

Gemini Perry knows her sister's accident didn't happen like the newspapers say. The truth has been buried and Gemini is just the woman to dig it up.

But the closer she gets to the man responsible for her sister's death, the blurrier the lines become.

Because someone wants the truth to stay dead, and they're willing to bury Gemini along with it.

Join the Legion newsletter to receive your monthly dose of SEEK YOU FIND ME.

www.annieande.com/seek-you-find-me

ARE YOU A MEMBER OF THE LEGION YET?

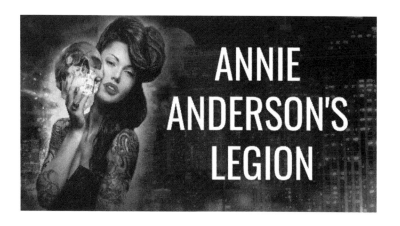

To stay up to date on all things Annie Anderson, get exclusive access to ARCs & giveaways, and be a member of a fun, positive, drama-free space, join The Legion!

facebook.com/groups/ThePhoenixLegion

ABOUT THE AUTHOR

Annie Anderson is a military wife and United States Air Force veteran. Originally from Dallas, Texas, she is a southern girl at heart, but has lived all over the US and abroad. As soon as the military stops moving her family around, she'll settle on a state, but for now she enjoys being a nomad with her husband, two daughters, and old man of a dog.

In her past lives, Annie has been a lifeguard, retail manager, dental lab technician, accountant, and now she writes fast-paced romantic thrillers with some serious heat.

Connect with Annie!
www.annieande.com

facebook.com/AuthorAnnieAnderson

twitter.com/AnnieAnde

instagram.com/AnnieAnde

amazon.com/author/annieande

bookbub.com/authors/annie-anderson

goodreads.com/AnnieAnde

pinterest.com/annieande